Oasis

Oasis

A NOVEL

Laureen Vonnegut

COUNTERPOINT
A MEMBER OF THE PERSEUS BOOKS GROUP
NEW YORK

Books published by Counterpoint are available at
special discounts for bulk purchases in the United States by
corporations, institutions, and other organizations. For more information,
please contact the Special Markets Department at the Perseus Books Group,
11 Cambridge Center, Cambridge MA 02142, or call (617) 252-5298,
(800) 255-1514, or e-mail special.markets@perseusbooks.com.

Designed by Trish Wilkinson
Set in 12-point Goudy by the Perseus Books Group

Library of Congress Cataloging-in-Publication Data

Vonnegut, Laureen.
    Oasis : a novel / Laureen Vonnegut.
      p.   cm.
    ISBN-13: 978-1-58243-360-8 (alk. paper)
    ISBN-10: 1-58243-360-7 (alk. paper)
      1. Women—Fiction. 2. Self-actualization (Psychology)—Fiction.
3. Sahara—Fiction. I. Title.
PS3622.O676O26 2006
813'.6—dc22   2006023004

10 9 8 7 6 5 4 3 2 1

Things don't happen,
it depends on who comes along.
—Paul Bowles

1

Sahara Sins

SHE TUMBLED ONTO THE GROUND AND SHUT HER EYES TIGHT against the unforgiving Sahara sun.

Gypsy bitch, he yelled.

He slammed the car door, the motor roared and her face was stung with sand propelled from the tires. She lay there on the ground until she could no longer hear the engine in the distance. No crying, she told herself, no crying.

She opened her eyes and cried anyway. Miles and miles of flat pale sand interspersed with a few tenacious bushes. Tire tracks in the sand, but no road, no sign of civilization. Far in the distance loomed the Atlas Mountains. Behind her was a tall, chain-link fence laced with weeds and shredded plastic. The fence enclosed a pile of stones and a mud structure that had partially collapsed and now tilted in odd directions. Mounds of sand obscured the carcass of an old truck.

Fucking Arab, she whispered.

The desert was so bright, it was impossible to think. Under her arm she found her sunglasses bent into an irregular shape. She put them on.

A faint sound murmured in her ears. She thought the wind was playing tricks until she saw the black gleam of the Land Rover heading back in her direction, a cloud of dust unfurling in its wake.

She ran to the fence, flung herself against it and crawled up to the top strand of barbed wire. One of her shoes dropped to the ground, the other wedged and stuck between two links. She looked behind her at the approaching car and grabbed on to the wire, for once glad of her height, which allowed her to swing her leg up, up and over. Metal barbs pierced both her hands. Her other knee caught on the wire, ripping open a gash of red skin. As she jumped down, her dress hooked on to the wire and a wide swatch tore from the hem, leaving a piece flapping on one of the spikes like a signal flag.

She ducked behind the pile of stones. A lizard stared at her indignantly before scuttling away. The Rover stopped in front of the fence and he stepped out, shouting.

Get in the car. Get in now, or I really will leave you to rot in the sun.

He hesitated a moment and kicked a spray of sand in the direction of the fence.

Your choice.

He walked around to the back of the car and reached inside. First he took out her makeup bag, the gold-tone one from the big store in London with all the lights, and threw it toward the fence. It hit a pole and split open, lipstick, shiny compacts, tweezers spilling into the sand.

He lifted her leather suitcase out and it flew open, dumping everything into the dust. He kicked her sweaters until they were gray, ground her sequined mules into pieces, ripped her silk underwear with his hands.

Next was the matching hanging-bag, which he unzipped, heaving each dress separately into the air. Sheer fabric caught in the wind and hung shadowlike for a moment, rhinestones glimmered falsely, bright colors became dim.

He spit in her direction, tripped over his robes and got into the car, reversing backward and forward over her suitcase several times before gunning the engine and taking off.

She emerged from behind the structure. The sun had beaten her hair into a liquid cap that dripped down her temples. A green silk sarong lay withered in front of her toes, she bent down and wrapped it around her head turban style. She rocked back and forth on her feet, the scorching sand burning the soles of her feet.

Her life had come to a stop. She could never get back into that car. And no one would ever find her here. So, she told herself, it would be here that she would die. Again. She had died twice before and was not afraid of a third death.

The sun had started its descent without abating its glare. Two large birds with hooked beaks glided over her. Next to the rocks were a rotted hose and a metal chair strung with a corroded plastic seat. She sat in the chair. It would be a fine place to die.

The lizard appeared again and twitched its head. Lili peered into its wide eyes. It stared back, its unflinching gaze and ancient wrinkles making it seem immeasurably wise. She watched the lizard a long time, hoping it would tell her something she needed to know. It lifted its body up and down in a caricature of a pushup, it took a step toward her, she leaned closer, craning her neck—again the roar of the engine echoed across the flatness.

The lizard disappeared. She jumped out of the chair and ducked behind the rocks. He threw on the brakes, the car spun in a half circle, encasing her in a film of dust. She could see his lips moving through the car window and seconds later he burst out, holding up her purse which was on fire. Her snakeskin bag from Italy. A wild moan escaped from him, he hurled the bag high into the air where it twirled like a crazed firework, spinning out the contents before dropping and extinguishing itself.

Lili, I know you're here, he said and grabbed the fence.

He started to climb up, but only the tips of his shoes would fit between the links and she knew he would stop because he was wearing his favorite hand-stitched loafers. A moment later he cursed and jumped down, lost his balance and sat ungracefully in the dirt. He took off a shoe and ran his fingers over the scratches.

Bitch, bitch, bitch.

His head jerked in an odd way that made her worried. A tremor shook his shoulders. What if he had a stroke or a heart attack?

Cunt, he choked out.

He was sobbing.

Stay away, she yelled.

Look what you've done to me.

I haven't.

Reduced to a broken donkey. A *crazy* broken ass. That's what I get for mixing with you, a foreigner, a non-Muslim. Oh, yes, I knew you were not a Muslim. You lied to me and tried to trick me and now Allah will punish both of us.

She whispered, I haven't done anything.

Damn you, get in the car, Lili.

Leave me alone.

Get in the fucking car. What do you think you're going to do out here?

Maybe I'll decide to die.

After all the money I invested in you, you turn out to be as stupid as I always thought you were. Fine. I'm going to leave you here to die, as you deserve.

A small snake emerged from the sand next to him, flicking its forked tongue. It blended perfectly into the sand, its back laced with muted triangles of brown and tan.

Look, she said, it's like my handbag you burned.

He turned to look and his face drained of color. She could hear his breathing, in and out, in and out, faster and faster. A high-pitched whine escaped from his throat, he jerked his hand away. The snake sprung into the air, striking him on the cheek, he knocked it away and it latched on to his hand. He shook his hand, the snake whipping back and forth through the air until it released its hold and landed with a puff in the dust. He sat back against the fence and watched it vanish into the sand.

Sweet Allah. Help me.

Why do you say that? Get up and go away, you'll be fine.

Baby, you've got to get me to the hospital.

You know I can't drive.

Please.

Why did you have to call me that?

What?

I told you there was one thing you couldn't ever call me, and you called me that.

I don't remember calling you anything. Please, the car.

Gypsy bitch. You called me a gypsy bitch.

I didn't.

You did.

It had nothing to do with you. Baby, you know I loved you.

Loved? Even if she didn't love him, why wouldn't he love her? She was eye-catching, graceful, educated—just as he ordered. She couldn't stand not being loved, especially not by him. Maybe it was her height, it was always her height he had hated. Why wouldn't he love her?

Loved, she said. Why do you say loved?

I'm dying, Lili.

Don't be silly, it was a little snake.

Little is worse. You are not small, but you are little. Bad little girl.

You made me bad.

Help me. I gave you everything.

His face was very swollen, one eye almost shut and a purple mound on the cheek, where he had been bitten. Maybe he was going to die. It wasn't fair for him to die first, this was her place to die.

Get up. You can't die here.

This is your fault. Climb back over that fence and help me.

He propped himself against the fence and dug into his pocket for his red pocketknife.

Are you watching? We have to get the poison out. I can't get it out myself. With the bite on my hand, I'll show you what you have to do.

He pulled a shoestring from one of his shoes and tied it around his forearm, already his hand had swelled into an ugly balloon shape. Sunlight glinted off the knife blade as he ran the tip across the purpled bump below his thumb and a red line the same color as his knife appeared. The red line split, widened and spilled over the back of his hand. He drew another line, so the two were in the shape of a cross.

I don't think that is the right thing to do, she said.

Shut up and watch. You're next.

He put his mouth to the cut and sucked at the wound. His neck convulsed and he spat out a mouthful of blood where it lay for a moment and then dried into a spot the color of rust.

Lili, sweetheart, come over here.

No.

Listen. This is a matter of life and death. Fhemti? Understand? You've got to come over here, do as I say and then drive me to the hospital. If you don't, you've killed me as much as this viper has.

Drive yourself.

What do you think will happen to you after I'm gone? You, alone in Morocco: no passport, a murderer. You will be beaten, jailed, raped, tortured.

I hate you.

We are in the middle of fuck-all. In no time, my eyes will be swollen shut and then where will I be? Blind and driving a car.

She stood up and wandered apathetically around the enclosure.

Maybe I can climb back over.

I'm tired, baby. Hurry.

The back of his neck looked pale and vulnerable. She felt a moment of tenderness for him. His head slid to the side and his eyes closed, he breathed slow and even. The skin around the bites turned a darker purple and looked almost black in the dimming light.

Wake up, she said. Wake up.

She pressed against the fence and screamed right into his ear, Wake up, you bastard. Listen to me. You don't know me, I've hidden myself from you. I lied to you. I fooled you. The me you know, is not me.

Several thick, gold chains hung around his neck, catching sparks of light from the lowering sun. She undid the clasps with her fingernails and slid the chains out from around his neck. The metal was hot and ran through her hands like liquid. One of the chains caught. She tugged, tugged again and it released, bringing with it several curly strands of black hair.

He twitched, flung his arm against the fence and she jumped back, but still he lay there, his hand now the size of a boxing glove.

Wake up. Oh God, I've killed you.

A piece of his shirt stuck through the chain links. She took it between her fingers and held on to it.

I'm sorry, she whispered.

2

Death of the Arab

I HAVE KILLED THE ARAB.

That one sentence brings great joy to me for two reasons. First it means that I am rid of his rapes and smells. His smell was the worst: sour, pungent, consuming. I still taste it in my mouth and feel it stick to the walls of my throat. I couldn't let him know how I felt, he would have discarded me and that would amount to slaughtering me in this Muslim land. I was tolerated because of who he is. Was.

Yet, I do not blame him for his rapes and smells. He has paid for it all and I am the receipt. In spite of my great height, he kept me and at times was proud of me. He did not treat me badly. I had food, nice clothes, I traveled in luxury. He beat me infrequently and desired me time after time. Still, I hated him.

The second reason is best of all, there is still a me inside of Lili. Even after Madame Mer and him. Even after all those years. His death has released me.

Me, who left Russia when I was twelve. Me, who was handed my personality, on a sheet of paper, by Madame Mer. Me, who was sold to the Arab at seventeen. Me, who was told I was lucky.

3

To Die or Not to Die

THE NIGHT WAS DARK, DARKER THAN SHE'D THOUGHT POSSIBLE with all the millions of stars in the sky. She could see nothing except an all-encompassing canopy of burning lights. The stars pulled her up into the soft center of their lights and the earth beneath her shrank to the size of her body.

She awoke in the cold. She curled deeper into the sand, but every grain was a tiny ice cube pressed against her skin. Her breathing pounded into the silence of the desert night. The stars, which had felt so comforting before, glittered remotely.

In the morning, the sky lightened slowly and the stars faded into the massive gray expanse. One second the world had been gray and black, and the next it was colored, as if someone had clicked on a great, rose-tinted light that warmed the air and brushed the desert with browns and reds.

There was more sky than earth. Always, in Casablanca, she had felt the earth to be the great power, the great force. In the desert, earth succumbed to sky.

He was gone. She looked carefully around. So was the car. It could have been a dream, except here she was in the desert, her possessions strewn about the ground.

As the sun rose higher, she could see where he had lain against the fence and, farther away, indentations from the tire tracks. Where had he gone in the state he was in? If he were alive, for sure he would kill her. She didn't mind dying here—that was her own decision—but she didn't want to be murdered.

To be murdered was her worst nightmare, not because of the death, but because it was the ultimate repression of her own will. Madame Mer had taught her she had no will. Enshallah, it was all up to Allah. She had had her will taken away for too long and now she chose to die rather than be killed.

Quickly the sun became hot, so hot it sent chills down her arms. She had been warned to stay away from the sun, it would make her ugly and men wanted flesh that stayed pale and soft. After all the years of staying out of the sun, she wanted to stay in it. She wanted her color to change, her skin to be rough.

I will die with the black skin of a Berber, she told herself.

Her stomach rumbled loudly and she automatically looked around to see if anyone else had heard. Not only was there no one else to have heard, there was not even the possibility of anyone on the scorched horizon.

The Spanish had been smart to relinquish this Saharan hell. Rio de Oro, river of gold, they called it. Years ago, they shrugged off abundant mineral mines and boatloads of sardines to let the desert nomads fight out territorial rights with the government of Morocco. Smart.

Next to the fence lay the scattered contents of her purse: two tampons, a cracked bejeweled mirror, a comb, a pack of bubble gum and half a chocolate bar.

She pounced on the chocolate bar and found it had partially melted into the sand. After a halfhearted attempt at picking off the grains of sand, she shoved the bar into her mouth. The sand crunched between her teeth, echoing in her ears. It didn't matter, the chocolate tasted glorious, heavy and creamy. She looked around for something else to eat. There was a tube of toothpaste underneath the burnt remains of her purse. The flavor was not as good as the chocolate and it became glued to the roof of her mouth when she had nothing to wash it away with. She sat in her chair facing the spot where she had last seen the Arab.

It was taking a long time to die. She was not used to so much daylight, in Casablanca this was normally when she slept. The skin on her arms had turned a fiery, blotchy red that pulsed if she touched it. Maybe it was too hot to die. She looked for the little snake to help her. Several persistent flies buzzed around her face trying to land, a small beetle struggled across a dune, but the snake was nowhere to be found. A bird circled far above.

Lili tilted her face to the sun and shuddered. She knew about the sun. Without water she would last two and a half days—in the shade. If she tried to walk out of the desert, she could walk five miles in the sun before she collapsed. She knew she should breathe through her nose and not her mouth, but it felt better to pant with her tongue hanging out. Sweat trickled between her breasts, down the back of her neck, along the sides of her face. She was sweating too much, losing what little water she had. She should wrap herself in her dresses to retain the water, she should sit in the shade. She stared at the bright colors and didn't move.

The rays of sun sucked all the energy out of her body. A loud rush hummed in her ears, dazzling fireworks exploded in front of her eyelids.

In her dream, cool fingertips soothed her burning skin, brushed her hair, circled her eyes, swept across her nose, ran lightly down her chest, trembling, barely whisking over her nipples and down, down past . . . until she heard a sharp intake of breath when her wounds from the barbed wire were discovered.

Someone felt pain for her wounds. How kind. She slit open her eyes, but the accursed sun shone straight into them and all she could see was the dark fringe of her eyelashes and an obscure figure kneeling over her.

Water was dabbed on her forehead, then squeezed down her throat from a wet rag. A trickle of water ran across her wounds, relieving the tightness. A slight breeze cooled her skin, lifting her body until she felt as if she were floating above the ground.

She was alone when she awoke. Torn strips from her hand-painted silk scarf had been wrapped around her hands and knee. Someone had gathered all of her dresses and laid them over the bushes to form a multicolored tent. Shade eased the heat of her skin, still the sun filtered through the thin material of her dresses. Next to her lay a robe and a jug of water. She tilted the water into her mouth and drank and drank, choking and swallowing, until the jug was empty. In the robe, she found a piece of bread and a handful of dates.

The dates were sweet and sticky with slivers of almonds dotting the sides. The taste was so good, the inside of her mouth ached and she felt light-headed. When she finished the food she remembered that if she wanted to die, she shouldn't have eaten.

She knew she could have reminded herself before she had eaten. It was tricky the way her mind made these decisions even though she had consciously decided otherwise.

The world tipped back and forth, she dropped into the sand and stared at her arm, which lay next to her face. Hundreds of bubbles had popped up on her skin. A tear dropped out of her eye before the bright desert turned black.

She knew someone was there, yet when she opened her eyes, there was no one. Days . . . nights, hot . . . cold, hunger . . . thirst, were all the same. Always she dreamt of the fingers running over her body, possessing her in unknown ways, touching places she never knew were there, until she was uncertain even if it was her own body she felt.

Who are you? she asked again and again.

No one was there. Confused by shivers and pounding in her head, she knew nothing except that there was nothing unless the fingers were touching her.

She found herself wrapped in the robe, her face still cool from fresh water. Footprints in the sand surrounded her, the same footprints continuing outside the fence, where in the distance she thought she could see someone in a dark robe walking into the whiteness of the desert.

Wait, she cried out. A small rough sound came out of her throat.

She stood and tried to climb the fence. There was no one to see and she knew the desert played tricks. The sand and sky moved as if she were on a boat in the middle of the desert. She held on to the fence to stop herself from tipping over into the sand. A hole gapped in one side where the fencing had been cut and stretched back.

She moaned. It seemed clear to her that she must go through the doorway. She must find the person who had saved her and demand that she not be saved.

To prepare for her venture into the desert, she selected her best Italian gown with invisible straps and a matching shawl that draped loosely around her neck. She could not find her mirror, so she applied her sand-encrusted makeup the best she could.

She stepped through the fence.

The footsteps led in the opposite direction from which she'd arrived. She put her foot inside the imprint, it was hard to tell the size as the powdery sand had already started to fall back into the hole.

She walked for a long, long time. Her legs ached and the blisters on her skin had swelled up again into hundreds of little water pockets. This desert was a deceptive landscape. At first glance, the sand looked flat and monochrome. Yet some dunes dipped into valleys and others sloped up only to fall away into precipitous slopes. A treacherous landscape. Landscapes revealed a lot about their inhabitants, she should be cautious.

When she looked back at the fence and her bright shelter, she found they were not far away. But they were at the bottom of a graduated rise and she a few steps from the top.

The moment Lili stepped to the top of the dune, a surge of air ran down the length of her body and she paused to savor the coolness

on her skin. She felt as if someone were exhaling a soft breath, starting at the tip of her toes and slowly moving up to the top of her head.

From below, the group of oasis dwellers saw a sky-high, white-
haired angel standing above them, arms outstretched, head tilted to
the clouds. A garment of shimmering material wrapped around her
body and flowed backward to form a pair of transparent wings. They
knew they were witnessing a monumental event.

The apparition rose to her tiptoes, momentarily airborne, and
then she dropped out of the sky, tumbling down the dune and sprawl-
ing flat on her back at the edge of the oasis. Her metallic gown re-
flected the sun in hundreds of tiny mirrored shards and the dwellers
had to shield their eyes when looking at her.

No one wanted to touch her. They stood back in a small ring, motionless with confusion. On closer inspection, their angel's skin was
deep red and blistered, her face painted garishly with smeared black
around her eyes, blood-dye circled her lips and a layer of shimmering
color spread over her cheeks.

She reached an arm up toward the sky, her dress shifted and sparks
moved in new directions. A soft moan escaped from her mouth.
They were stirred into action and carried her into the shade of one of
the women's tents.

The air surrounding Lili was thick and her head too heavy to lift. She
opened her eyes and found she was lying on a woven mat in a dark
room. Blades of dusty sunlight lined the floor. There were no movements within the room and when she was sure she could not distin-
guish any breathing inside the room, she leaned forward and peered
through a slit in the wall.

In front of her was a bedraggled oasis with an oblong pond in the
center and a group of dense palms that curved around in a protective
arc. Scattered along the perimeter were taller palms and below them,
at the heart of the oasis, the tents of the desert dwellers. At the far
end, a dozen camels were clustered, swishing their tails, flicking their

heavy-lashed eyes at flies. The water itself was not particularly clear, nor was it unusually opaque.

A group of people squatted under one of the tall trees. She counted five people: three women and two men. Two women were wrapped from head to toe in black, the other was dressed in a sassy red skirt. Some yards away from the group, a hooded man squatted in some bushes near the camels, watching the group out of the corners of his eyes. The red-skirted woman stood and walked toward Lili's tent. Lili lay back down and closed her eyes.

As someone entered the tent, she felt the air move around her. Lili lifted her eyelids slightly and saw the woman's face inches away from her own. Fierce features with two pugnacious eyes rimmed in shadowy kohl. Lips long and thin and equally portioned. A dark tattoo, an elongated diamond, sliced down the center of her forehead, ending between her eyebrows.

Sbah el kheer. Thank God you are here, in my tent, the woman said, her eyes softened and turned up at the corners. I knew, when I saw you, who you were.

Lili stared at her, willing her mouth to move. It took too much effort and she wondered if she were paralyzed.

You are here for me, she tapped the front of her chest, Ouma. She watched Lili closely, as if expecting Lili to recognize her. The time will come for you to help me, but you must not tell the others.

She poured water from a jug onto a cloth and draped it over Lili's head. She flapped her red skirt over Lili's body a few times and nodded determinedly.

The next time Lili opened her eyes, three people sat in a semicircle around her, Ouma and the two men: one, small and pale who wore a neatly tailored shirt, and the other, sour-faced with the lips of a cherub, dressed in robes and a weather-beaten turban. Lili's eyes darted from one to the other, had one of them given her the dates and water? Had one of them touched her? She stared into each of their eyes.

Midhat, she is the answer, the small man said.

The answer, Midhat repeated derisively. The answer.

She is looking at me, the small man said.

The cuffs of his shirt were frayed and a sliver of his bony elbow poked through a hole. Lili looked at him standing over her and she could see exactly how small he was, as small as she was tall. She liked him immediately.

Three pairs of eyes regarded her with curiosity.

What is her name? Midhat asked.

Ouma shrugged. She never spoke before.

We have been blessed. Whether you say she is from Allah or I say she is from Jesus Christ, it is a miracle.

Midhat's chin twitched in a nervous spasm. You Christians attribute everything to miracles.

She has been sent to help me, he said and crossed himself.

Midhat creased his brow and said, Only God can help man.

Ouma, what language does she speak?

Ask her yourself.

The small man inquired, Spanish?

Lili tried to respond, but the *si* came out as a hiss.

French?

Arabic?

English?

See her eyes? She understands them all. She is educated.

Lily opened her mouth. I want to die, she said in a ragged voice. She felt good saying this out loud and having witnesses for her declaration. She repeated her words with more strength: I want to die.

They stared at her, their eyes wide.

Was it you? Lili focused her gaze on Ouma. Was it you?

Ouma shrieked and darted out of the tent.

You have a fever, Midhat stated. Your journey has been long and now you have made me late. And I am never late.

He puckered his Kewpie doll lips and leaned out of the tent. Fatima, Raja, he bellowed. Fix some food and prepare my bags.

As soon as Midhat's head was out the tent, the small man leaned toward her, keeping his eyes on the doorway.

The Sahara covers one third of Africa, he said quietly to Lili, speaking out of the edge of his mouth. It is the size of the U.S., the dunes are ever-moving. Please, I am Gabriel, help me. Tell me—

A light layer of sweat appeared on Gabriel's pale forehead and he clutched his hands together. His lips were delicate and trembled slightly, his tongue darted out to moisten the corners. He glanced back at Midhat and leaned closer, holding out a tin container of water. Lili drank until her stomach felt heavy and her head felt light.

Please, he said, tell me where to look.

I don't—

Please.

I . . . what are you looking for?

My mine.

She heard him say "mind." She feared that she had landed in the midst of a covey of crazies who had been chased away from the villages to live in the middle of the desert. Who else would be living here?

Your mind . . . I cannot say.

A hint, just a small hint, to help me.

Midhat stood facing them in the doorway. I must leave, he said. The camels are waiting.

Gabriel whispered, I've been searching for so long.

Gabriel, what are you mumbling? asked Midhat.

Please . . .

Lili sighed. It is nearer than you think.

Nearer than I think? He looked around frantically and then stared down at his feet.

Not there.

Midhat pushed him away from Lili. Stop bothering her. You're as crazy as that lunatic in the bushes.

Gabriel turned to Lili. I am not crazy, he said.

You Spaniards were thrown out of the desert twenty-five years ago.

Spanish territory, the Rio de Oro. We left peacefully.

Those mines were not Spanish, anyway.

Of course they were.

Even if you found your elusive silver mine today, you would either have to fight Morocco or the rebels for it.

What about my paper?

You come from a small village in Spain, you don't understand the ways of countries like this.

I understand this. Gabriel withdrew a skin bag from around his neck and pulled out a tiny piece of paper which he unfolded with extreme care.

You are wasting your life.

This is my life. He shook the paper at Midhat.

Crazy. Midhat pursed his Kewpie lips. Crazy.

Gabriel raised his hands and twisted them in Midhat's direction as if he were strangling him and stalked out of the tent.

Midhat looked Lili up and down. The black pores on his nose could have been freckles except for their darkness and their too-even spacing. Heart-shaped lips on such a face were disconcerting.

Listen, my little fallen angel, he said.

He shifted toward her and she could smell the decay under his robes. A bright red vein had burst in the corner of one eye, looking as if it could drip down his cheek.

I am not a fool like the others, he continued. I do not believe you are anyone special. You are an outcast and a troublemaker who found us by accident. You are dangerous.

I did not ask to be here.

Lili sat up and kneeled on the mat. Midhat looked up and down the length of her, calculating her standing height and stepped back, repulsed.

You cannot stay here. You will only bring trouble. I have enough trouble with the nomads. No one wants camels anymore, they shepherd their herds around in fancy blue vans. Who ever heard of a nomad in a van? He twitched his chin and focused on her. Be gone by the time I return tomorrow. Enshallah.

Don't worry, I will die soon.

The vein in his eye swelled. You do want to die!

I do, I do. I just don't want to be killed.

What does it matter?

It matters.

It does not matter, it will be the same outcome.

One is a decision, and the other is not.

Either way, it is the will of Allah. He glared at her and strode out.

Lili was left alone in the room. Giving it closer examination, she saw that it wasn't a room, but a tent made of thick brown wool. In fact, almost everything in the tent was made of wool: the roof, the walls, the pillows, even the floor was made of woven rugs with tassels. She stood up and her head brushed the coarse roof. A shower of fine dust wafted down on her. There was nothing to remind her of civilization except a cracked mirror set in a shiny silver frame propped against the far wall.

Outside and across the oasis, the two women in black, only their eyes showing above their veils, prepared the meal. Shouting orders and insults at the shorter one, the larger woman sat in the shade fanning herself while watching the shorter one run around frantically. The large woman was bigger than anyone Lili had ever seen, round as a mosque, she was a mosque unto herself.

It was impossible to tell which woman was shouting except that the large one's veil puffed out with each syllable.

Lili sat down and put her head in her hands. These people thought she was something she wasn't. They expected her to help them. If they knew she was a murderer, they wouldn't be so eager to let her remain at their oasis.

There was a sound behind her and the light clearing of a throat. Lili turned to see the smaller of the two robed women. Her startling blue eyes peered over her veil, light as the sky, with eyelashes so thick Lili could count them if she wanted. Naughty gold slippers peeked from beneath her black skirt. She looked to the right of Lili, rather than at her. Her eyes were so pale they would have blended into the whites had it not been for the black outline encircling them. She was not actually a woman, Lili decided, more of a young girl.

Your eyes, Lili said.

Yes, she said and lowered her gaze.

Is the world brighter?

It can be bright. Her voice was slightly mottled from the veil.

Do you see things differently?

She looked at Lili with her brilliant eyes. I have a terrible power in my eyes. Since I was a child, everyday things are different for me. I see what they really mean.

Lili looked around the room to see what the girl could be seeing differently, what she, Lili, could have missed, what meaning was hidden in the rough walls. All she saw were the geometric shapes woven into the rugs.

The morning of the day you arrived, the girl continued, I watched a bird fall from the sky and land right on top of my head. At first I looked at the sky angrily, then at the bird. A pale green bird the color of ripe melon. It was still alive, I gave it some water and laid it in the shade and I realized I had seen a sign. Something was going to happen . . . later you arrived. Most people would have dismissed the sign as simply a worn-out bird falling from the sky, but I knew it was something more. Feel my head, there is a lump here.

Lili reached her hand out and beneath the heavy black fabric and damp spongy hair, there was a round swelling.

You fell into our oasis like a great shimmering bird, just like the green one this morning. You do understand, don't you?

Lili felt an affinity to the green bird tumbling out of the sky. She nodded.

I knew you would, the girl's eyes crinkled with a smile.

A voice bellowed from outside the tent, Raja, Raja.

That's me, she sighed. Raja.

Raja lifted up an edge of the tent and peeked outside. The fat woman in black glared in the direction of the tent.

I have to go, she said. Or Fatima will stick me with her pins. Come, you must eat with us.

Outside, the evening wind began to blow a fine spray of sand over the crests of the dunes. A broad sheet of stiff leather tied between two fig trees formed a windbreak, but it could not stop the dust. The dust dimmed everything. Dust on the palm fronds, dust on the water, dust in Lili's eyes that formed an opaque film across her vision.

A chipped clay pot lay nestled in a pit of smoking coals in front of an open tent set up for eating. Inside, on the right, sat Fatima, the ponderous woman in black. Her robes were decorated with thin metal pieces, reflecting streaks of light. The light danced in front of Lili, hurting her eyes. She realized Fatima's robe was covered with dozens of safety pins, of all sizes, starting with small ones at the top and growing until the largest ones ran along the bottom of the hem. Fatima stared aggressively at Lili.

Raja, she called, not moving her eyes from Lili, feed us.

Steam rushed out when Raja lifted the lid of the pot off the fire, infusing the air with the aroma of harira. Gabriel was served first, in one side of the tent. A striped blanket hung from the middle, ceiling to floor, dividing the two sides. Then a bowl for the man in the bushes, which Ouma carried to him. He pulled his hood further down around his head, leaning over the bowl until his face was hidden.

Poor Gabriel, Ouma said when she returned. Look at him.

Gabriel sat on his side of the tent, bowl in his lap, his small form made smaller by the background of the desert. He stared morosely into the white horizon.

You are always causing problems. The men have always eaten there, said Fatima. And we have always eaten here.

Midhat is gone. Ouma looked around the oasis. We can take down the blanket tonight.

What? Fatima spit out the word. You know this cannot be.

Raja, do you mind? asked Ouma.

Raja flicked her blue eyes toward Gabriel and continued filling the clay bowls. I don't know, she said in a tiny voice.

It is forbidden, Fatima declared. Next you will invite the lunatic over.

Don't distract me, Gabriel called from behind the division. I am watching the dunes. The desert is a slow moving sea.

He watches the dunes, Ouma said to Lili.

For what?

She shrugged. He says they move.

Migrate, Gabriel said. They migrate.

The heavy aroma from the harira made Lili's tongue feel thick and she had to swallow several times. I don't eat meat, she said.

Raja's eyes widened. There's nothing else.

The harira smelled better to Lili than anything ever had before. Bean soup with meat and vegetables. It reminded her of her life in Russia, before the fall of Communism, when it was still possible to buy meat. If she had eaten meat in Russia, why didn't she eat it now? There were all sorts of reasons for not eating meat: health, protest against the treatment of animals, pure dislike of it . . . none of them applied to her.

She must have been told to be a vegetarian. Madame Mer again. It was difficult to know what was really her and what had been created by others. She would have to question everything.

Yes, Lili said, I would like some. She reached for one of the bowls and held it up. I am no longer a vegetarian.

No, no, sorry, not that one, Raja said and took the bowl from Lili.

Fatima and Ouma each took a bowl and a wooden spoon.

No, please, Raja tugged the bowl from Fatima's hand, not that one.

Fatima reached over and jabbed Raja with one of her safety pins. What has happened to you? Have you lost your senses, stupid girl? Now give me that bowl.

Raja rubbed her arm with the pin prick. No. I think that is Lili's.

You have the mind of a flea. Why should she have this one?

I don't know, maybe it was not that one. Raja looked at all the bowls. Now I don't know. Allah have mercy on me.

Raja, Fatima raised her voice, we will eat. Bi-smillah.

The soup was so good that Lili's jaw throbbed. I'm never going to die this way, she said to herself. Obviously, the way to die was not through starvation, but through a different means. She would look for the little snake or perhaps a scorpion.

Halfway through her meal, Lili felt the hooded man watching her. She stopped chewing and looked around, immediately his eyes shifted to the ground. She went back to eating and felt his eyes on her again.

That man, why is he in the bushes?

He is a lunatic, Ouma explained. He stays in the bushes.

Why?

He looks after the camels.

What is his name?

He doesn't have a name.

No name? Why not?

He doesn't speak.

That doesn't mean he's a lunatic. Lili thought about why someone wouldn't speak. A throat injury, missing teeth. Maybe he doesn't have a tongue she suggested.

He eats his food.

Lili wiggled her tongue inside her mouth. Do you need a tongue to eat your food?

Nonsense. Look in his eyes. The man is a lunatic. Fatima swallowed her last bite, chewing with great relish and belching. You are almost learning to mix your spices, she said to Raja.

Fatima's mouth opened and she gasped toward the sky, her lips snapping open and shut. She pointed a shaking finger at Raja.

Poison, she rasped. Her djellaba quivered like black jelly, her veil fell away from her mouth and she crumpled onto the ground, the lower half of her face exposed for the first time in many years. Several long black hairs trailed from her chin like whiskers on a camel.

Fatima raised her hands to her eyes and cried, My eyes are dark. The desert is black, Allah have mercy.

4

Moonlight on the Oasis

Madame Mer told me I was lucky: He is a Western-educated man and you will be his third wife. You will not be kept like his other wives, locked in their house, you will be allowed to live in freedom.

Freedom? He kept me in his flat in Casablanca. When he was gone, I had a watchdog named Yamal, an ugly Moor with dark teeth and pits in the skin of his cheeks. He went everywhere with me.

Sometimes the Arab brought me with him on business trips. He would disappear for several days and leave me with the watchdog, who stuck to me like a starving street urchin.

One day in Marrakech, however, I managed to lose the watchdog in the market and when he found me, he beat me. He used his rubber-soled shoe so the marks would not show. He said that if I did it again I would die, because so would he, if the Arab discovered I had gone off on my own.

Madame Mer, so called because of her odor, created me. She handed me my character in the palm of her hand. Likes and dislikes, smells and looks. She told me how to talk with my eyes, stride with my shoulders, and charm with my hands.

I was raised in a prison. I called it a prison, Madame Mer called it a French finishing school. It had high walls and no one was allowed inside but the girls. And the men on visiting days. We were taught to be gentle, compliant and above all a virgin. The men required un-blemished "wives," and Madame Mer was known for her fresh-faced, well-behaved virgins.

He bought me when I was fifteen, the girls were not sold too early. I was the last of my age group, not because of my face. There was something about me the men shied away from. Maybe these men could sense something in me, my bones waiting to grow, my body having a hidden agenda of its own. Smart men, it could have been them lying in the sand.

Madame Mer said, He wants you to entertain his Western friends, so you will be educated. Not many of our girls have this opportunity. You are lucky.

Originally he had selected another girl, Iris, who was petite and had the yellow eyes of a cat. But she couldn't learn all that he wanted his wife to learn. He called her an imbecile and made her learn the word *stupid* in twenty languages and write it a thousand times on the black-board. I was taught five languages, geography of the world, quotes of famous men, flattery at its most insincere.

What Madame Mer didn't account for was that I would keep so much of myself hidden inside, tucked away in the farthest reaches. Slowly, slowly, though, since the death of the Arab, I am returning. I feel something uncurling inside my body. Something supple, some-thing resilient—something me. She would not be happy to hear this.

When I went to live with the Arab at the age of seventeen, Madame Mer told him I had grown all I would grow. Her last words to me were: Stop eating. I grew until I reached almost two meters. By then the Arab had discovered that my height fascinates men. First they are repelled, then they are drawn to my length, the sheer num-ber of millimeters of skin.

I suppose Madame Mer was right, I am lucky.

5

Boom

IN THE MORNING, MIDHAT RODE BACK INTO THE OASIS, SWAYING on the back of his camel, laden with two baskets of supplies. Half a dozen camels trailed behind him, tied together in a train. He looked around and spotted Lili sitting in the shade before him, her green dress spread about her feet in a small glittering puddle.

You, he said. You are still here.

I am waiting.

Wait elsewhere. And where is your robe? He narrowed his eyes and looked away. Have you no shame?

I have no robe.

Lily stared at his saddle. It was very odd, intricately tooled and painted with bright colors. The horn of the saddle protruded upward in front of him, rising between his legs into the shape of an upside down duck foot. He looked silly, as if it were a misshapen penis. She smiled.

He glared at her. Why have I not been greeted in the manner I deserve? Where are the others?

Ouma is in her tent, Gabriel is searching for his mind, the lunatic is in the bushes—

Where are my wives?

Fatima—

Raja is here, Raja said walking out of her tent and pointing at herself. Please, Midhat, I must talk to you.

Midhat looked beyond her and frowned. What is all that raised dust behind the camp?

Gabriel.

He squinted at the dust. What is he doing now?

Doing what he always does.

What? Not there?

Yes, she told him where his mine would be.

She . . . what?

She told him his mine was nearer than he thought.

He roared at Lili, You told him that?

I—

He slashed the rope that connected the camel train and tore off in the direction of the rising dust. The camel galloped across the dunes, grunting with each stride, Midhat beating at its flanks with a cane whip.

Sand shifted in one of the camel's footprints. Lili stared. The sand shifted again. Something lay hidden under the sand. Something sand colored. A dull patterned back emerged and then disappeared except for one black marking. A snake. Just like the one that killed the Arab. This would be her way to die also. It was only fair.

First one foot, then the other, she slowly moved toward the snake. Loud shouts, from Gabriel and then Midhat, arose from across the dunes. Ouma ran out of her tent, her red skirt the only spot of color on the horizon. She headed toward the shouts, Raja following behind, holding her djellaba up with one hand while trying to keep her veil in place with the other.

The snake disappeared entirely. Lili ran to where the sand had shifted and threw herself on the ground, digging desperately, sand falling in as fast as she threw it out.

Someone grabbed her arm and held it tight. The lunatic stood above her, his eyes scowling out from the depths of his hood. They were light brown and candid. Direct and inquisitive. People in the city had the same eyes, he wasn't a lunatic, he belonged in the city. He was out of the bushes and no one was here to see.

I have already died twice before and I am not afraid of my third death Lili said. Leave me alone.

He drew something in the sand with his curled fingernails: the word BEN. He pointed at himself. He had a scraggly dark beard that turned copper when the sun hit a few strands of it.

You're not crazy, are you?

He shrugged and then cackled to himself.

A sharp crack cut through the air, followed by a screech. Lili pushed the lunatic out of the way and ran, following the footprints in the sand until she came to the others. They were standing near the fence where Lili had originally arrived. Not a trace of her belongings or the Arab remained. Raja clutched her robe to her chest and cried. Gabriel crouched holding a shovel to his chest and Midhat stood some distance away posed as if in midstep, leaning on the butt of a long gun.

Gabriel's legs gave out and he sat heavily on the ground, staring straight ahead, repeating, I didn't know, I didn't know.

What? Why are you standing there like a rock? Ouma asked Midhat.

A click, he said in barely a whisper.

Click, Gabriel said with a shudder.

Click? Lili looked from one to the other. Click?

A click. The click of a land mine.

Sweat ran down Midhat's face and dripped off his chin. Slowly, slowly he raised his arm and wiped it away.

I thought my mine was there, Gabriel said, so I kept digging. He was trying to shovel the sand back in faster than I did and he took a step and . . .

What was the bang? Ouma asked.

He shot at me, said Gabriel.

I shot nothing at you. If I'd shot something at you, I would have hit you.

Liar, Gabriel said, liar.

It is only I, a man of God who tells the truth at this oasis. I shot near you. To scare you.

If you're standing on a land mine, Lili said, why aren't you dead?

I am dead.

You're not dead.

I am dead, as soon as I move my foot. Midhat's head dropped down and his shoulders shook. A sob escaped from his chest. Oh merciful Allah, save me.

Then let me die. I will take your place. Lili started toward Midhat.

No, no fool of a girl. Stay where you are or we will all go up in one big explosion.

Raja wailed and held her arms out to Midhat.

No, no, stay away from me. Idiots. Fools, all of you. Raja, look what you will be left with if I die. You will be alone with a crazy Spaniard, a lunatic, an outcast and a whore.

She's not a whore, Ouma said.

She is a whore and you are an outcast. If she is who you think she is, tell her to tell me what to do. Midhat looked at Lili. They think you are a jenni from the oasis, Aisha Qandisha. If this is true, you must tell me.

A jenni? Me? Tell you what?

What must I do to save myself?

You said I was dangerous and to leave. Why should I tell you anything?

You see, he said to the others. She is nothing.

Lili looked at Midhat standing in his ridiculous position. I don't believe you've stepped on a land mine.

Of course I've stepped on a land mine.

Here?

Don't you think I know? There are more than a million land mines in Morocco—this is one of them.

The wall-of-land-mines is on the border of Algeria. That's where you'll find your million land mines.

If there are a million land mines, who's to say one didn't get planted out here? Anyway, we are not far from Algeria.

Land mines are not animate, they cannot walk or crawl all the way out here. Someone would have had to put it out here in the middle of nowhere.

This is a war zone, don't argue with me. There are rebels everywhere. I know that I heard a click and I know what I heard. Why am I surrounded by idiots? Where is Fatima? Where is my Fatima?

Her eyes . . .

Gabriel cleared his throat. She is ill.

Ill? Midhat stared at Raja. Fatima is ill? Stupid, stupid girl. What have you done to her?

Raja took a step back. It was an accident.

You killed her, Midhat accused.

Not killed, Raja cried. She covered her eyes with her hands and pointed to Lili. She said she wouldn't eat meat and would not take her portion and then we had too many dishes and Fatima grabbed one and by then I was not sure which dish was which and I had to leave the decision to Allah.

I entrusted this to you. I put my faith in you.

And my faith is in Allah.

Look at you, Midhat said to Raja in a low hoarse voice. You are why I owe so much. You are why I have to work so hard. I am a slave to my own trade. Camel trading used to be a respectable job. Now, nobody wants to buy a camel. But a camel can go twenty to twenty-five days without water, even less in the winter. Trucks need water in their radiator and petrol in their tank at all times. What's wrong with a camel? I paid your father twenty-two camels and what do you give me? Do you give me the child I so badly want? Nothing. Barren as the desert. All those camels for nothing.

Have pity. It could have been me eating the powder.

Better you than my first wife, stupid cow that you are.

Stupid cow, Ouma muttered. Look who's standing with one foot in the grave.

Lili thought about the food. She thought about Fatima going blind and reaching for the sky.

Raja, you tried to poison me, Lili said.

Oh, please, it was not my decision.

You tried to kill me.

Midhat will tell you. Midhat, tell her.

Lili squinted at Midhat. I told you I was ready for my third death and I told you I would die, but that I did not want to be killed.

And what did I tell you? I told you it was all the same. Whatever happens is the decision of Allah.

Then he will also decide your fate, Lili said and turned her back on him.

Where are you going? Why do you speak to me with such disrespect?

Loss of fear. It is an advantage of the nearly dead.

Allah, Allah, Midhat called out to the encroaching darkness, I implore you. I will devote myself to your needs. I will change my life.

You're worthless, all of you. He swung his head toward Gabriel. Mindless Spaniard, living on dreams. Why don't you go back to Spain and make babies? You are wasting your life here, drying into a hard white pole.

With who? Who is going to make babies with me? I have nothing to offer.

You are nothing. He turned to Raja. And you, you must give me a son. If you do not . . . if you do not, you should be afraid.

Raja stumbled after Lili and grasped her wrist. Please, she whispered, tell me what to do.

Lili snatched her arm from Raja and put her hands over her ears.

Raja dropped at Lili's feet. You must help me. I know you are the one, the green bird. Remember the green bird. My eyes saw it for what it was. Give me another vision.

Midhat ranted on, raising his fist to the sky, not noticing his audience was deserting him.

. . . And Ouma the discarded, Ouma the abandoned, the rejected.

You must try a different means, Lili said to Raja.

Raja looked horrified, then resigned. Yes, she said. Thank you.

Midhat's voice trailed after them . . . Cowards, where are you going? Come back and listen to me. Maybe your thick heads will learn something . . . Don't leave me to die alone in the dark, come back. No—all of you deserve to die. I will kill you all if you don't come back. Not one of you with half a brain. Don't—

6

Death Through the Bosphorus

MY FIRST DEATH OCCURRED AS I WAS THRUST THROUGH THE BIRTH canal, out of my mother's warm body and into the world. My mother also died, but her death led her into a different world from mine.

The false mother who raised me, told me my real mother was a gypsy. As if it were a disease she had saved me from.

The second time I died was very much like the first—I was thrust into a new life: from Russia to Morocco. My false mother sold me. We were so poor in Russia after Communism fell, I don't blame her. Our neighbors were selling plates from their kitchens, shoes, lamp-shades. Anything to survive.

The lady next door, who used to buy buns in the neighborhood bakery where my mother worked, knew someone who knew someone who needed help in their house. Far away from Russia.

When there was no more flour for the bakery and nothing left in our home, my mother bathed me, pulled my hair back into a smooth ponytail and knocked on the lady's door. The lady was not surprised to see us. Her mouth stretched into a smile, but not her eyes. "A big house," she said in a loud whisper, "with stuffed couches and furniture that shines like a mirror."

A woman with vivid red hair and the shiniest shoes I'd ever seen took me to Odessa, where I boarded a ship that crossed the Black Sea.

I remember being hungry, the woman hadn't fed me in our two days of travel and the sea air filled me so I felt I never had to eat again. As the ship traveled down the Bosphorus, much as I had traveled along the birth canal of my mother, I emerged on the other side and everything was changed—I died and was reborn in the Marmara Sea.

I've never had control over anything in my life. This time I will have control over my next death.

7

The Russians Are Coming

Out of the desert came not Midhat, but two men. Two men perched awkwardly on their camels, black suits rumpled and gray with dust, hair so short their scalps glinted beneath. Above their heads they held faded umbrellas with broken ribs. The men arrived with white beaming smiles, teeth like bleached desert bones and hands widespread in greeting.

Raja scurried to the back of a tent and peered around the corner. Lili fingered the tiny fist-sized bag necklace around her neck that held the gold chains and thought about escaping the oasis. She felt the weight of the chains in the palm of her hand. These men could help her. If she left, she could die in peace, her own way. She could be rid of the oasis and its crazy inhabitants.

As a woman, Lili knew she shouldn't be greeting strange men, but curiosity won over propriety. Besides, that was a rule Muslim women had to obey and if she weren't Muslim, it didn't apply to her. She stepped forward and smiled.

Salaam aleykum, the men cried in unison.

Aleykum salaam, answered Lili, Ouma and Gabriel.

The two groups stared at each other for several moments, particularly the men staring at Lili, who was wearing her orange silk gown from France with the large hole burned near her ribs, where her flaming bag had landed.

We have come a long way to find you.

Lili cringed. To find her. The Arab had sent them to find her. She took a wide step back.

You have been looking for me? Ouma said.

You and all of you.

You have come all this way for us?

Yes, to bring you news.

It is a long way.

Nothing is a long way.

How did you know we were here?

The Lord our savior sent us.

Lili relaxed. The Arab wouldn't have sent religious foreigners after her. That sort of cunning would be beyond his abilities. If he were alive.

Have you come to save Fatima? asked Raja, from around the corner of the tent.

Yes. They looked at Lili. Their eyes were shrewd and perceptive. They had already condemned her of an unforgivable sin. Are you Fatima? they asked.

No, Lili said. No.

Fatima is in the tent, said Ouma, pointing to the tent.

The men awkwardly dismounted from the camels, one man sliding to the ground and landing in the dust. He rose and brushed himself off. They immediately strode toward Fatima's tent.

No, stop, Raja cried. You cannot show men into the tent of a woman.

We are men of God.

From inside the tent, Fatima began to howl. Lili had never heard such a sound, which brought images of devastation, torture and misery. The men stopped and put their hands over their ears. One looked as if he might cry with her.

We have a message to bring you, he shouted, when Fatima took a breath. You will be saved.

The howling stopped. They stared at the tent as if a devil were inside.

One of them nudged the other. As soon as you read this, he said, you will be saved.

He said it in a voice that did not believe its words.

I cannot read, Fatima said. I am blind. A trembling hand appeared from the tent and pointed wildly to a palm tree. It was her, her with the blue eyes, she said. She tried to kill me.

The men turned to look at Lili. She stepped out so they could see her.

Are my eyes blue? She tried to kill me, too. It was her. Lili pointed behind the tent to Raja, where her head vanished.

One of the men put a hand over his mouth and the other looked confused. Is this true? he asked.

No, said a weak voice from behind the tent.

Because it is in direct opposition to what the Lord says, to try to kill another human. Are you familiar with the Ten Commandments?

Commandments?

From Moses, you must know them: Thou shalt not kill.

But I didn't kill her. See, she is still alive.

You must love your mother.

She is not my daughter, Fatima said, praise to Allah.

She is not my mother. We are both wives of Midhat.

Two wives of the same man? Oh, no. No, no, no. You must take this book and you will be saved.

He thrust the book into Fatima's outstretched hand. Her hand retreated with the book.

Lili lay in her tent and listened to all the noises in the night. There was the slight sound of someone's foot landing on the sand, the grains compressing and shifting. Later there was a muffled exclamation in a foreign tongue and then fast footsteps, the flapping of robes. Lili looked at Ouma, who lay sleeping, and crept to the door. Loud voices were raised at the other end of the oasis and candlelight flickered. A figure in a djellaba darted around the back of Fatima's tent. It wasn't Ouma—Fatima wouldn't move from her bed—so it was Raja creeping around in the middle of the night. And talking to the missionaries. Raja converting to Christianity. Midhat would banish her to the far reaches of the desert.

Lili was asleep when she heard a voice calling, Baby, baby . . . save me. She sat upright. The Arab. He was alive.

He wanted her to think he was dead. He was alive and watching her. He used to try to trick her like this. He would spy on her and then ask, what did you do after breakfast? or what did you have for lunch today? and then it would casually come out in conversation that he knew the exact answers to his questions.

She rushed outside to find everyone else already there, staring, not at the Arab, but at Midhat, who sat in the middle of the tents. His foot stuck out in front of him, wrapped in his turban, his hair hanging in strands around his shoulders.

The sun had not yet risen and colors were beginning to seep back into the world as the night evaporated. There was enough light to see that Midhat's turban was soaked with blood.

Allah akbar, I have had an epiphany, Midhat announced. Allah has shown me the way. I have a plan, everything must change. He opened his arms wide and smiled. From now on, we will help others less fortunate than ourselves.

Lili recoiled. This was frightening, sour-faced Midhat smiling and talking of helping others. And where was the Arab? She peered into the shadows suspiciously.

I am a changed man, he declared. We must band together.

For what?

We must help those less fortunate than us.

Who might they be? inquired Lili.

Those who are persecuted and prosecuted.

He wiggled his turban back and forth across his foot. People of the desert.

There are no more people of the desert, they were in the refugee camps for over twenty-five years—they're not refugees anymore, they're not nomads, what are they?

I mean the others.

The rebels? Gabriel looked dubious.

Call them what you like. Midhat struck the ground with his fist. We will all help them.

How?

That is to be revealed later.

You are talking about fighting the military, said Gabriel.

No, not the military, the Russians.

They glanced sideways at each other. Lili felt sick. Either he was crazy or he knew everything about her and he was going to reveal her story. He was toying with her, making her panic. When they discovered she was a murderer, she would be chased into the desert and left to the missionaries. She had to die before her death was taken out of her hands.

Midhat, said Ouma, what has happened to your foot?

It was a small price to pay for my life and my epiphany.

It's bloody.

Gone. *Bam*. Blown up.

An explosion? I didn't hear anything.

No? And such a big explosion. How could that be? You heard it, Raja, didn't you?

I . . . I don't know.

Oh, yes, huge explosion.

Maybe there was a noise, Raja ventured.

Is it gone? asked Ouma. Your foot, Midhat, is it gone?

Toes. Some of them.

Raja motioned toward his toes, We should take care of them. But she didn't approach him, she sat back on her haunches and stared.

Midhat suddenly noticed the tents at the other end of the oasis. What? *What?*

They are missionaries, Gabriel said.

What do they want?

They want to help us. To save us.

From what? Where are they from?

America.

A whisper of a voice came from Fatima's tent, She killed a chicken.

Midhat sat up straight. Fatima?

Her voice said again, stronger, Raja killed a chicken. I heard her and it was not for us. She went to them.

Midhat stood and limped stiffly to Fatima's tent, trailing the strip of his bloody turban.

What now? Midhat's outraged voice surged out of the tent and filled the night sky. Fatima, what is this?

Midhat, have mercy, I am blind.

Of course you're not, the sun's coming up now.

She tried to kill me.

Kill you? Stupid fool girl, oh what has she done to you, Fatima?

There was a long silence that filled each of them with a terror, like a night terror, in which there is nowhere to turn and an overwhelming paralysis strikes every muscle.

A square fluttering object came hurling out the door, followed by Midhat.

What do I find? Fatima with no eyes, and this. A Bible. A Western Bible. What else did you give them? Was it just a chicken or was it more? He examined Raja closely. Yes, I see, there was more.

A whine escaped from Raja and she shut her blue eyes tight.

Look at them—they camp at the wrong end of the water. The food will be stolen from them in a matter of hours, if not by the jackal, then by the fennec. Raja, you must steal back whatever you gave them, before the jackal gets it.

Steal it back? It was to help them with their mission. What about being good and helping people?

Stupid Americans. They are richer than anyone else and they are always asking for money.

But how can I steal from missionaries?

I don't care how you do it—just do it.

It was nothing. It was the sick chicken and only a few dirhams.

Do you think we have money to throw in the wind? He leaned toward Raja with his lips curled back. Go now.

Raja's eyes turned to two blue pinpoints. She ran off into the fading shadows. There was silence as Midhat stared off into the whitening sky. Everyone else gazed at him and shot quick glances at each other.

Midhat focused his eyes on Lili. You, where's your robe?

I told you, I have no robe.

Well, get one. Ouma, give her a robe.

Ouma eyed Lili up and down. I'm not sure I have one big enough.

A robe is a robe.

Inside the tent, they lit candles and Ouma rummaged through her leather chest. She found a robe and thrust it at Lili.

Lili pulled the robe over her head, and as she did, a scent wafted through her head. It reminded her of civilization: coffee instead of tea, juice instead of goat's milk, wine and French cheese in the afternoon, drinks on the roof of her apartment before dinner at Ma Bretagne. That's what it reminded her of, it reminded her of Casablanca, where she had lived with the Arab. It was her perfume from Paris she used to wear.

What are you doing? Ouma said and yanked the robe the rest of the way over Lili's head.

Lili looked down at herself. The robe fell all the way to her ankles.

This is my robe, she said, staring at the colors in the flickering light.

It was the robe she had packed in her suitcase, the one the Arab had flung into the air before he met the snake.

Your robe?

Yes, mine.

You didn't have a robe.

I did. It was . . . lost.

This is *my* robe, Ouma asserted.

Do you wear it?

It is for special occasions.

Where did you get it?

It was a gift.

Recently?

No.

Yes.

No. Not recently. Do you want it or not?

The robe had been a birthday gift from the Arab and she didn't want to be reminded of either the Arab or her birthday. No, she said. Do you have another?

Lili hoped it hadn't been Midhat who had found the robe at the fence and given it to Ouma. That could mean that he had been the one touching her, she couldn't stand it if he had been the one. The thought of his squat fingers on her skin made her throat constrict. But he had wanted her dead, so why would he have saved her when she was dying of heatstroke? Even diminutive Gabriel would be better, or the lunatic. At least the lunatic with his missing tongue would be forced to keep the secret. She would watch him more carefully.

Ouma held out a different robe. Lili slipped it over her shoulders and tried to wriggle it down her body. Ouma grabbed the front and pulled. With a slight snapping of seams, the robe tugged down. The hem brushed Lili's knees. It fit snugly in a very un-Muslim way.

Maybe the other is better, suggested Ouma.

Lili sighed and slipped her robe back on again. Yes.

Shoes?

Lili looked down at her feet. She wore her silver lamé sandals with the heels that had snapped off in the sand. The arches were broken, the lamé long gone. Bright beads had been fixed to the straps, but had mostly fallen off, leaving dirty dabs of glue. At one point, the shoes had been top-of-the-line couture sandals.

What is wrong with my sandals?

They are for shepherds.

Lili tried to imagine shepherds mincing around in her sandals. She looked at Ouma dubiously.

Here. Ouma handed her a pair of the pointy leather slippers.

Lili held them next to her sandals. Given the state of her sandals, her own footwear did look shabby and unrefined next to the slippers. And the size was close enough to Lili's small feet. Even so, Lili handed Ouma back the slippers, she would keep one part of her old self just to remind her that she was not really from the desert.

Fine, no shoes. Underwear, then.

She put a shoe box in front of Lili and whisked off the lid. Inside were dozens of tiny folded panties and bras. Geometric designs, abstract washes, bold solids. All silk. From Paris. The last thing she expected to see at an oasis in the Sahara.

All from my lover, Ouma said as she closed her eyes and ran her hands through the fluid softness.

Lili gazed into the box. She remembered when the Arab had bought her a set of underwear in Paris and how even he had been shocked at the cost. Your lover must like you a lot.

My lover loves me. He lives for me and I for him. Which do you want? A matching set? Something different?

Lili sifted through them, there were dozens of pairs, all styles and colors. She chose several, which the Arab would have hated: simple, sheer and white with high French-cut legs. He hated white underwear of any kind and favored minuscule G-strings. So, this was what it was like to make decisions on her own. She loved it.

Those? They are ugly. How about these?

Ouma dangled a pair of purple tiger-striped underwear from her fingertips.

No, no. But thank you, Ouma.

Thank my lover.

Lili slipped a pair on and at that same moment, outside the tent, one of the missionaries shouted, spasibo Bog, God save me.

Lili peered out of the tent. Midhat ran over and grabbed Lili's arm, dragging her outside.

What? he asked. What did they say?

The temptress was in my tent again. She's back, the missionary cried. She's back. They are devils here. Lord save us from temptation and deliver us from evil . . .

They said they saw someone, Lili said.

Now what? Now what do they say?

They are reciting something from the Bible. A prayer.

Oh no, not at my oasis. Midhat waved his arms excitedly. This is a Muslim oasis. No Christian prayers allowed. They must leave.

A small hunched-over form darted in from behind them.

Here, Raja said. Here is what you wanted.

Midhat looked at what she held and roared.

Another Bible. This cannot be so.

He unstrapped his sword and limped toward the missionaries, Raja tugging on his sleeve. He slapped at her as he would a fly.

The chicken is gone, Raja said. The chicken is gone, take the money. Here. The money is in the Bible. Look. Look.

Midhat continued around the oasis almost forgetting his missing toes. The missionaries had already spotted Midhat with his sword and were frantically throwing their goods into the camel packs. By the time he reached them, they were leaping onto the camels, heading off into the desert trailing blankets and ropes and a pot that banged against a camel's hind leg.

8

Sex with the Arab

SEX WITH THE ARAB WAS NOT PLEASANT. SOMETIMES IT LASTED forever and sometimes it was so fast I was barely aware of him, but no matter the length of time, or city, or position, he never kissed me. I am twenty-two and have never been kissed. Unless I count the time Rosa at Madame Mer's tried to kiss me and I think that was more of an accident than anything else.

Due to my lack of kissing, I must be obsessed with lips, as they are the first thing I notice on a person. In Morocco the women wear veils and the men wear beards. Veils are a disaster for lip watching and I can only get a glimpse of what lies beneath a beard. I loved going to different countries for that reason, I could see everyone's lips. The French have the most expressive lips, the United States the most diverse, the Portuguese the sexiest.

What happened within that fence, as I lay dying from the sun, was not sex. It was pleasure. Quite a different experience.

If I were a good Muslim girl, I would have been offended by the touching and wouldn't have wanted anyone to touch me in such a way. But I have to remind myself I'm not a good Muslim girl, I'm not even a Muslim girl.

The only time I remember the Arab losing his desire for me was in Sweden. It had nothing to do with him or me, it was purely the weather. Cold weather.

Not the sort of cold I remember from Russia, where the sky was as gray as it is blue here and when the sun showed itself it was special and everyone celebrated. That's the good kind of cold.

The cold in Sweden hurt. The Arab made us stay in the ice hotel where everything is made from ice: walls, furniture, even bed. It was supposed to be a marvelous experience. I would never have thought that I would be begging for this cold again. Any cold. Ice, drafts, chills, frost, all of those words bring such an intense longing for something other than the inferno of this desert.

In Sweden my skin smarted, my head ached. Eyes stung as if sand-paper had been grated across them, mind numbed to distraction, shivers that shook my entire body, fingertips white then purple, lips peeling in hard little crusts, skin tender as new skin under a blister.

Then the Arab lost his desire for me and didn't want to leave the bar. He stayed there and drank and drank while I went to the room and shivered under the down comforter.

During World War II, when Hitler was running his human experiments, one of them was to plunge a man into ice water and leave him until near death. Then the man would be pulled out of the water and resuscitated by different methods. It was found that the quickest way to revive someone, to raise a man's body temperature, was through sex. I did not mention this to the Arab.

After the Arab's drinking spate, we left the next day for the Bahamas. He blamed the quick departure on the loose morals of the Swedes. I didn't bother to point out his own. Besides, I knew the Arab needed heat to make his blood flow.

Sometimes I think that if someone does kiss me, I will be his forever, no matter who does it. Sort of like the young ducklings that follow whatever they see first out of their shell and accept it as their mother.

9

Midhat's Epiphany

THE GRAY FIGURES OF THE MISSIONARIES MELTED INTO THE lightness of the morning sun as it rose over the dunes, casting strange shadows in the valleys. One of the shadows moved, a desert mouse and then another, more slowly.

A snake, said Lili.

Ouma looked. The oasis is infested.

Good. Lili separated herself from the others and began to edge toward the snake.

It is good, Ouma said. If it weren't snakes, it would be rats.

The mouse focused on the oasis, undoubtedly thinking about the seeds under the palm trees, the snake thinking about how good that mouse would feel in its stomach, and Lili, concentrating hard on her third death: her chance to thwart Midhat, to deny him the satisfaction of surrendering her and to escape the Arab once and for all.

As soon as Lili neared the snake, it vanished. This time she moved slowly, methodically, feeling through the sand, to the right, to the left and down until a cool smooth surface brushed against her skin. Her fingers curved around the snake and she yanked it out of the sand. She shook it in the air. The snake hissed and writhed, stronger than she had imagined. She stared into its flat eyes, it did not have the wise eyes of the lizard.

A hand grabbed her arm, seized the snake from her. The snake doubled back and sunk its fangs into the other hand. Lili whirled around. Midhat held the snake in his fist. She could see the two little holes in his hand where the snake had bitten him.

You're crazy. Now you're going to die.

I have saved your life.

Why? I want to die, you want me to die. Why?

It is not time for you to die.

Why not? And who saved me before? In the desert?

The others did not reply. They backed away from Midhat who was brandishing the snake wildly in the air.

You've stolen my death. Lili lunged for the snake. Give me that snake.

I saved you. Midhat held it out of her grasp with one hand and snatched her arm with his other hand. Your life is mine. I have plans for you now.

He pinched her arm with the strength of a falcon. Tell me you will live. Tell me.

Lili tried to pull away. He tightened his grip and brought her close to his rank breath.

It doesn't matter, she said. Now you will die and your plans will never be known.

I will not die and you will not die. He waved the snake in the air. If Allah wishes it so, it will be. Tell me.

He increased the crush of his talons. Lili glared at him. It seemed impossible to die here. Maybe it was not the right time for her third death. The last two times she did not remember having to fight so hard to die.

Midhat watched her carefully and released her arm.

You will live, he said.

She vowed that if she lived, she would not live here, not at this forgotten oasis with the most idiotic people she had ever encountered. She would escape the Arab. Dead or alive, he threatened her. She would not allow herself to be found a murderer: jailed, beaten, raped and tortured as he said she would be. She would find someone to hide her, to buy her a fake passport, to sail her across the Strait of Gibraltar.

She had the Arab's gold chains to pay her way. In addition, she would find the fingers that had evoked such a response in her. Yes, she would live.

She pushed up the sleeve of the robe to see the red marks Midhat's fingers had left, long thin marks starting to turn blue. Remarkably clawlike.

Midhat held the snake victoriously in front of him and declared, Take note of my power.

Midhat, Raja shrieked. Kill the snake at once.

It is already dead. I have been bitten, he said as he moved toward them. And the viper has died from my blood.

He is trying to kill me, Raja jumped back and held her hands out in front of her.

You see, now I am powerful.

He is trying to kill me, I know.

At this Raja began to cry. Lili couldn't see her mouth opening, but she wailed and her eyes flooded with tears until they were shiny pools waiting to overflow.

No, Midhat waggled his finger at Raja. I don't allow tears here. Water is the blood of the desert. Now, he said, I want you to listen— I have a plan.

He settled himself on the ground, sticking his foot out in front of himself, adjusting the bloody turban with a sad expression on his face. He made sure everyone saw him staring at his foot. His fist clenched the limp snake as if it were a staff.

My toes have been sacrificed for the good of all. We must be good, we must help people . . . do good, be good.

Gabriel cleared his throat.

Do you understand? Midhat asked.

No, said Gabriel.

We must steal from the Russians.

The oasis was silent except for a small whine that escaped from Raja.

It is a perfect plan. First we sell the Russians what they want, then steal it back. We will end up with everything. It is the will of Allah.

Russians, Midhat? Gabriel snorted derisively. In the desert?

They are everywhere.

I don't believe these Russians exist.

Midhat looked around the group, his eyes resting on Lili the longest. Her entire body tightened, she was glad for the protection of the robe. Here it was—Midhat would tell them she was a Russian, and a murderer.

Minerals, he said.

Lili relaxed. Obviously, Midhat had lost his senses.

Phosphates, salt, Midhat continued. And silver mines. The Russians are here to protect them. They have invested billions of dollars in them. Billions.

Maybe they have your mines, Gabriel, said Ouma.

No, he said doubtfully.

You want us to attack them? Raja's voice rose into a high whine. Fight the Russians?

No, not fight them, steal from them. Like with the missionaries. We take back what is really ours.

Then what?

Midhat looked down at his bloody foot for a moment. He smiled his wide grin again. He looked at Lili.

She will tell us.

What?

You will help us save our land from the Russians.

The Russians are not taking our land, Ouma claimed. Morocco is.

Forget about the government. We will all save the desert. *Everyone.*

We?

All of us.

Me? Lili asked. A Robin Hood of the desert?

Who?

Robin Hood.

They looked at Lili, puzzled.

Never mind, she said.

This is completely insane, Gabriel said. Why should we help you? You will see.

No.

You will be convinced. Midhat bared his teeth in an attempt at a magnanimous smile.

Midhat, Raja said, you are talking about stealing.

There are certain people who deserve to be stolen from. They are thieves and bastards, I know.

Thieves and bastards—it was the Russians he was speaking of, her people. Were they still her people? The Berbers and the Bedouins and the Arabs were not her people, so the Russians must be her people. He was talking of stealing from her people. Did he know of her background? Was he trying to trick her into saying something?

This was a test. If Raja can steal from the missionaries, each of you can steal from the Russians.

I was caught, Raja protested.

We need practice, he said decisively.

10

Unbalanced

I AM SIX FEET TALL. I TELL PEOPLE I AM FIVE FOOT ELEVEN. I LIE, but in my mind, I don't feel so tall. I feel petite and small enough to disappear. Fat people have told me that there's a skinny person inside them, it's denial any way you look at it.

When I left my village, Odessa Novaya, at the age of twelve, I was not so tall, not such a freak show. Gangliness in a young girl can be attractive, as she grows older it changes to awkwardness. Madame Mer did everything to stunt my growth: gave me coffee to drink, cigarettes to smoke, held back food, all to no avail.

I was destined to be one of these permanent fixtures at Madame Mer's, sad girls who scrubbed the bathrooms and ironed the others' dresses. The Arab saved me. It was pure luck that his first choice, Iris, failed because of her stupidity.

By the time I left Madame Mer's there were two Lilis. The other girls called us Grande Lili and Petite Lili, with the names switched, so mine was Petite Lili. Madame Mer didn't have much creativity with names for us, they were always flowers and her list of flowers was limited.

The Arab took me home when I was seventeen and Madame Mer promised him that I had stopped growing. She was wrong. Month by month my bones grew. My legs extended, my torso elongated, my neck reached for the sky.

The Arab was appalled by my growth and threatened to return me. He told me I was a malformed deviant, but by then, I had become a curiosity among his friends and clients.

I always feel a little unbalanced. This is because all of Madame Mer's efforts concentrated on my feet, which stopped growing long before I reached my full six feet. Other tall people have big feet—I've seen them—whereas mine are child-sized. The Arab liked this about me, he would proudly bring my small feet to everyone's attention.

One time, a girl, Daisy, was returned to Madame Mer because she couldn't tolerate her "marriage." Daisy informed us of the horrors of marriage and of the fat, cruel man who bought her and who asked her to wear underclothes that left her nipples uncovered and hit her with a cat-o'-nine-tails when they had sex. Madame Mer discovered what Daisy had told us and the girl disappeared for a few days. She returned silent and nonresponsive and was now treated as one of the maids, scouring and ironing. No one called her Daisy anymore and soon after, a new Daisy appeared.

After the Arab realized what a showpiece he had, he decided not to return me and began to make me wear high heels and stand tall, shoulders thrust back. Men like to stand next to me because my breasts are at eye level.

In the desert, I wear flat shoes and no one mentions my height. I wear a djellaba all the time and can crouch down if I want to be short, even curl into a little ball with my arms wrapped tightly around my knees and become a pebble in the desert. The flat vastness of the sky and desert makes me feel small and insignificant, a blissful feeling I've never felt before.

11

❖

Heat and Hairs and Bathing

THE WORST THING ABOUT THE DESERT WAS THE HEAT. CHOKING,
lung-crushing, brain-numbing heat. Sheer heat that annihilated any
action or thought Lili may have been considering.

The best thing about the desert was the bath. Gabriel had dug a
channel from the oasis to a small rocky basin so clean water could be
let into the basin when they bathed. He also strung large rectangular
camel hides around the basin so there was complete privacy. The
women could wash, scrub and polish their skin for hours if they
chose. It was the only time of day Lili felt dust free.

Her lips continually tasted of salt. They cracked and bits of them
peeled off. She chewed at a piece, crossed her legs and shifted further
into the shade. It was almost time for her evening bath. She would
pay a lot of money to step into an air-cooled room and soak in a
frothy bath full of French salts. Not that she had a lot of money.

She reached inside her robe and took out her tiny evening bag,
which she wore every day around her neck, even when she bathed. It
used to be a chic glittery little purse. Now it was a soiled cotton sack,
metamorphosed from purse to pouch, the beads long scattered.

She turned the bag upside down and the Arab's gold chains spilled
onto the sand. They lay there dull and thick, looking frighteningly
similar to the snake, as if a forked tongue would suddenly flick out.

She knew they were worth enough money to buy her way out of the oasis and away from Morocco. Far away.

Caught in the chains were several hairs. She pulled one out and stared at it. Thick, curly and black: the Arab's hair. A shiver ran through her arm, she dropped the hair. It lay on the white sand accusingly. Above her the palm leaves rustled, the last shadow of a bird darted across the dunes as the sun set. She felt he was near, watching her, waiting. Quickly, she pulled off the other hairs, dug a hole and dropped them in.

Lili lit a dozen candles and placed them around the perimeter of the bath. Ouma built a small fire to heat the metal barrel of water. Once the water was hot, they would tip the barrel into the basin to form a large oval bathing area. In the desert, there were no bars of soap or bottles of shampoo, instead she dripped a thick honeylike soap over her body and rubbed a handful of rocks into a lather for shampoo. Ouma had shown her how to mix salt and mint to clean her teeth.

Lili pulled off her robe and threw it over the wall. She carefully unzipped her midnight blue evening gown and held it out in front of her. Although the gown was creased and gritty, the silk threads still shone in the light. She shook the gown, clouds of fine dust circled her.

The dust, Lili said, how can you stand it?

Dust?

It was true, Ouma didn't seem to notice the dust. She always looked as though she had just stepped out of the bath, as though her skin never felt the wind or collected any residue from the desert.

Lili sat on a flat rock and lifted her hair so that the evening breeze ran along her neck. Ouma sat across from her. She had a graceful body with small muscles and luminous skin. Lili wondered what it would be like to be Ouma, with her compact body so low to the ground. Would the Arab have still liked her to stand tall and parade around his friends?

Tonight Ouma wore a pair of black-and-white underwear with a pseudo-animal print. Lili unwound Ouma's smooth braids and poured a scoop of warm water over her hair. Ouma tilted her head back and grinned. With her black tattoo and gleaming teeth, she looked primal, ready to tear a piece of raw meat with her sharp incisors.

There was a rustling in the corner of the tent.

Who's there?

Raja moved between the hides. Me, she said.

This is a surprise. You are honoring us.

No, I mean, yes. With Fatima being blind, she won't bathe out here anymore, only in the tent, so I thought tonight …

There is plenty of water.

Raja undressed slowly, facing the walls. She turned around and sat on a rock next to Lili. Raja had a cherubic body: curved shoulders and thighs, circular breasts, high arched ribs.

Raja, your veil. Or maybe you've forgotten we are all women.

It is not possible.

Of course it is.

I cannot take it off. Don't ask.

I will ask. Don't be such a donkey, you look ridiculous.

Please, I cannot. Midhat—

He is not here.

He will know.

What are you hiding?

Hiding? What about her? Raja pointed to Lili and wagged her finger at the pouch hanging from Lili's neck. What is she hiding?

Ouma eyed the pouch between Lili's breasts as if seeing it for the first time.

Let her keep her veil, Lili said. Everyone has secrets.

I have no secrets. Ouma shook her shoulders in annoyance. Everyone else has them. You and you and the lunatic and Gabriel and Midhat, who has the biggest secret of all, with his crazy plan.

Lili poured another scoop of water over Ouma. The kohl ran around her eyes in a dark mask.

The snake has made him lose his mind, said Lili. There are no Russians in the desert. She held her breath, waiting for Raja and Ouma to respond.

I have never seen Russians, Raja said. Maybe Midhat is . . . confused.

His mind was lost before the snake. He cannot possibly expect us to turn into pirates, bandits and thieves. Russians or no Russians. He cannot force us to do anything.

Lili let out her breath. No one knew. She looked at the blue bruises on her arm and thought of the viper bite he had taken for her. With a combination of manipulating and cajoling, mixed with a dose of fear, surely Midhat could be persuasive. She plunged her hand into the syrupy soap and dripped golden strands down Ouma's back.

Raja scrubbed at her feet with a rough rock. His craziness is saving him from the venom, otherwise, he would surely die.

Poor Midhat, said Lili. He has lost both his toes and his mind on the same day.

He belongs in Bervechid. Ouma looked disgusted. House of the insane.

When Midhat says everyone must help him, do you think he is talking of everyone? asked Raja. Including the lunatic?

His name is Ben, said Lili.

What?

Raja clutched Lili's arm. She could see the wide outline of Raja's open mouth through the thin veil.

Ben.

How would you know?

He told me.

He couldn't have.

The whites of Raja's eyes showed and her hand grasped for something in front of her. She sagged against Lili, her body a dead weight.

My god, Lili said, easing Raja to the ground. She fainted.

They crouched next to her and Lili shook her shoulder. Raja, Raja?

Ouma held a gourd of cold water over Raja's face and trickled it onto her forehead. When she didn't respond, Ouma emptied all the water onto her face. Raja opened her eyes and spit out a mouthful of water. She propped herself up on her elbows, looking from Ouma to Lili.

What happened?

You fell over.

Maybe . . . I must have fallen asleep. Fatima is awake all night cursing me. She does not know night from day and soon, neither will I.

We were talking about the lunatic.

Raja's eyes fluttered back in her head. Her veil slipped to one side. Ouma looked sideways at Lili.

Again? So you think she's ill?

No, she faints easily. One time she thought she saw the face of her father in a sand dune and fainted right off her camel.

They both looked back at Raja and the corner of her face that was showing, one pink cheek with a tiny black mole.

Nothing unusual, said Ouma.

There must be a reason she won't show us her face.

Exactly.

They looked at the veil. It revealed a small portion of her mouth.

Okay, Lili said.

With two fingers, Ouma slowly tugged on the veil until it slid below her chin. Nothing horrible about Raja's face: a small snub nose, bowed chin, a small pink mouth with light fuzz above her upper lip. A small mole the size of a fleck of pepper marked the inside corner of her mouth. Raja's eyes opened and focused on them.

I am sorry, she said and smiled nervously.

As soon as she smiled they could see why Midhat did not want anyone to see her without her veil. She went from a striking beauty to a cute mouse. Her upper lip protruded over her sharp front teeth, which stuck out in a V-shape, giving her the stunned look of a desert rat.

Oh, Raja, said Ouma.

Raja looked from face to face and she realized that they were staring at her without her veil. She flung herself face down in the sand and wailed.

He will kill me. Midhat will kill me.

Stop, he won't know a thing.

Now you know I am not beautiful, you know why he hates me. He paid so many camels for this face and now I can't even give him a son.

Remember, Ouma said, Allah does not look at bodies and appearances. He looks at hearts and deeds.

The day after our wedding he returned me to my father and demanded his camels back. My father asked him not to shame me, for it would be the end of my life.

Midhat saved your life?

They agreed that Midhat would take half of the camels back and I would never show my face again. Midhat agreed to pull out the ugly teeth and I had one year to give him a son. I have one month left. Then he will return me, and my family will be shamed. The most beautiful girl returned in shame.

I didn't know. Raja covered her mouth with her hand. I thought I was the most beautiful girl in all of the Sahara. Until he looked at me on our wedding night and told me the truth.

She sat up and took the veil from Ouma and tied it around her face.

So why are you afraid of the lunatic?

He doesn't speak, Raja's veil fluttered rapidly. I know he doesn't speak.

No.

You said you know his name.

He wrote it in the sand. B-E-N.

Did he write anything else?

Like what?

Anything.

Only his name.

Then he doesn't speak. And he stays in the bushes. Her eyes searched Lili's and the color slowly returned to her face. I cannot believe any of this, she said.

Why does this matter to you?

I cannot trust you.

Why should you mistrust me? I should mistrust you, Raja. You're the one who tried to kill me. Lili took advantage of Raja's reclining position and leaned close to her eyes. Why did you want to kill me?

He told me to.

He?

He said you were dangerous.

How?

I don't know.

And now he wants me alive.

What is he planning? Ouma shrugged. We will have to watch and wait.

Don't you see? Raja said. He is collecting lives.

12

Call Me Gypsy

THERE WAS ONE THING I ASKED THE ARAB NOT TO CALL ME. Gypsy. And what did he call me? Gypsy.

After my mother told me my real mother was a gypsy, I used to sneak behind the village to the gypsy camps and watch them, hoping to see my mother. The splendid mess of them: colored laundry, mismatched socks, dingy underwear hanging from every bush. Some of the gypsies lay about on greasy straw mattresses. A little brown bear was tied to a tree. Two black-and-white horses fed on a pile of straw. Always a scampering of feet, laughing and singing.

There was a woman I thought was my mother. A small pretty woman who couldn't possibly have given birth to me.

One day, a boy caught me spying and he pulled me into the center of the camp. They gathered around and talked, solemn and then shouting. I stood, head held high, looking around to see if I saw her. She was standing off to one side, leaning against a tree trunk. She had dark, dark eyebrows and half a smile on her face. A young girl stood next to her, clutching her skirts.

The girl gave a shriek and ran toward me, arms flung out to her sides. She reached me and stood looking up, moving her lips as if she were telling me a secret. I smiled and leaned over and in one quick movement, she ripped a curly ribbon from my hair and ran back to the woman. Everyone laughed.

I stood so still, hoping they would see I was one of them. Instead, a man wearing a red shirt like a woman's brought forth two snarling dogs. He told me I had one minute to run and then the dogs would come after me. Everyone clapped and hooted, and he said, "Run." I stood there, still hoping they would recognize me, but in the end, he shoved me in the direction of the town and I ran.

Once, the Arab asked me if I would like to go back. I said, "Madame Mer does not like girls to be returned." He had leaned closer and said, "I was not talking about there, I was talking about where you originally came from, Russia. Don't you miss it?"

"I don't remember it," I said.

"She told me you were Russian royalty. I know that is a lie, but you must have come from somewhere."

"I come from Russia."

"A village, a camp? A gypsy camp. Yes, you have a wildness about you, like a gypsy."

"Don't say that."

"Are you commanding me?" he asked, looking amused.

That's when I said to him—never call me a gypsy.

That was years ago, and he had never called me a gypsy until that day in the desert. Interesting what sort of debris an argument can dredge up.

13

Ouma's Secret

DURING THE WORST HEAT OF THE DAY, LILI LAY ACROSS HER BED and dripped water from a sea sponge over her body. When she was finished with that, she stepped outside the tent, as she did every afternoon, to see if the evening breeze had begun to blow. Nothing. Every shade of brown lay in front of her: coffee brown, cinnamon brown, caramel brown, peanut brown—and she was starving for something other than brown bean soup. Heat bit at the corners of her eyes, pounding from above until her head lolled to one side.

A battered blue truck with a sideways lurch drove up to the oasis and stopped. Curls of dust spun into the air. A big man in Western clothes stepped out of the door, slamming it closed with force. He leaned back into the truck through the open window and pushed on the horn several times.

Lili folded her arms and said, Stop it.

But she said it playfully. Perhaps he was her ticket out of the oasis. His eyes flickered in her direction and he continued with the horn. This was the first time she had tried to flirt with a man since her arrival at the oasis.

She took a step closer. Hey, she said.

He pressed the horn again.

She clicked her tongue and realized why he was not paying attention to her—she was wearing these damn robes. Raja walked out of the tent. He glanced at Raja and then looked again.

It's true, he said.

What? said Lili, looking from him to Raja, who now stood, eyes downcast.

She is the one. They say she is the most beautiful in all of Morocco.

Raja looked at Lili in panic, her hand fluttered up to her veil and tugged it higher. Lili narrowed her eyes. She wanted to scream at him, You can't even see her. She's covered from head to toe except for her eyes. What about me? We're a perfect height, you and me. We'd be a good team. Take me away from the gritty ludicrous oasis.

He pulled his eyes away from Raja, he looked around as if he'd forgotten what he came for. A camel belched and the man's eyes refocused.

Where is Ouma? You, he pointed at Lili and hit the horn with his other fist. His forehead glistened in the sun. Go find her.

Lili whirled around with her nose in the air and walked to their tent. The tent was empty. She turned to go, but heard a slight noise in a corner. A hiss.

Ouma?

Psst. You see, we are not all saints.

Someone crouched in the darkness, a robe pulled over his head, voice distorted behind the cloth. The tent seemed unfamiliar, as if she had stepped into unknown territory.

Ouma?

We all have our terrible secrets. This is mine.

Ouma, is that you?

An indrawn breath. Lili.

There was a long pause of silence broken only by the persistent sound of the horn. Lili stepped closer to the door, ready to dart into the bright sunshine and familiar world, as unpleasant as that world may be.

He is why I am here. Ouma uncovered her face.

Ouma, you frightened me.

Why are you so frightened, Lili? What is your secret?

Lili tried to see her expression in the dark. Did Ouma know? Was Lili marked as the murderer she was? Unless, of course, the Arab was still alive—then she would not be a murderer. She would be about to be murdered.

Secret?

You wouldn't be here if you didn't have a secret.

I'm here because I want to be.

I don't believe you.

So Ouma didn't know and she was still safe. Or maybe Ouma was toying with her. The horn continued to sound.

This man is determined that you see him, Lili said.

This man . . . I am here because of my husband.

This man?

My husband.

Ouma, you had better talk to him.

Oh, no. No, no. Please. I left him. Because of the way he smells.

Ouma, this man is serious.

So am I. He smells wrong to me. My breath stops in my throat. My stomach runs in circles, I can't be near him.

A bath?

No, you don't understand. That has nothing to do with it. It is the smell of his skin. When he is clean, when he has just bathed, it is the same.

Lili remembered the repulsive smell of the Arab and how it would catch in her throat. Would she be able to smell Ouma's husband the way she smelled the Arab? Or was a man's odor particular to each woman, explosive or weak, repugnant or intoxicating, each combination of man and woman a new mix of chemistry?

I'll talk to him. Don't worry.

Lili walked back outside and faced Ouma's husband. Sweat ringed his armpits, a single drop fell from the end of his chin. She sniffed the air to see if she could smell anything: camels, dust and lingering smoke from the morning fire.

She is not here. Would you like me to say who called when she returns?

He stepped toward her, faster than she'd thought possible for such a big man, and grabbed ahold of her hair.

Ouma, he bellowed. I know you're here and if you don't come right now, your friend will not have a hair left on her head.

Ouma, Lili screamed, get the hell out here.

There was a flapping of the tent and Ouma emerged.

Ouma, the man said. Ouma, you must come home.

Let go of her.

He looked down at the fist of hair in surprise, but didn't let go. Lili smelled his sharp smell. It reminded her of the Arab, the day he died, it was the smell of fear. Ouma's husband was afraid of something. Other than that, he didn't smell any different from most men she had smelled. Certainly, he did not have the horrible smell of the Arab.

We are waiting for you—your child and I—we are waiting.

Ouma tore at her robes, but would not go any closer. I will not, I know what you will do.

Get in the truck.

It is not possible. You made me leave.

All is forgiven.

No. She took a step backward.

Yes, please, we need you. Your child misses you.

This is a trick. If everything is all right, let go of her hair.

He released Lili and again with astonishing speed, bolted to Ouma, who collapsed in the sand when he seized her arm. You little whore, stand up. Get in the truck.

In a panic, Lili ran around the oasis, forgetting the heat, searching for help. Ouma's screams grew louder. Around the back of Midhat's tent, she found Midhat reclining and smoking.

Quick, Ouma needs help. Please.

He merely looked at her.

She is in trouble.

I know she is in trouble, I can hear her.

Please.

She is not my wife.

What does that matter?

She is not my problem.

He will kill her.

It is the way. I cannot interfere or he will kill me.

We have to help her. Do something. Stand up, damn you.

He crushed out his cigarette and shook his head. Lili stomped her foot in the sand and ran off.

Ouma's husband had her near the truck and was trying to open the door. She kicked at him as Raja tugged ineffectively on his arm like a scared fledgling bird. The back of his shirt was drenched in sweat. Lili held her breath, wrapped her arms around his back and heaved. He didn't budge. Not only that, he managed to fling open the truck door, shoving Ouma half inside.

A horrible, ear-splitting wail started. On the level of a screeching cicada. Or feedback on a microphone. Ouma's husband tried to hold on to her while putting both hands over his ears at the same time.

Fatima stood in the doorway of her tent, the unreal sound emitting from her mouth. She was even holding her veil up. Her pink tonsils, the color of cherry blossoms, quivered with the effort or Lili wouldn't have believed the sound came from Fatima.

Make her stop, said Ouma's husband. Allah, preserve my sanity.

Ouma scooted to the other side of the truck and raced across the sand, tripping on her robes and stumbling to the ground. On hands and knees, she crawled into the tent. Midhat appeared from around the tent, leaning on the cane stalk he had taken to carrying with him. Fatima closed her mouth.

Now, Midhat said, would you like a cup of mint tea?

Ouma's husband took his hands away from his ears and glanced wildly around him. Midhat continued walking toward him and talking.

It is the best, khamsa njoum, five-star tea.

Ouma's husband nodded in a dejected way and made his way to one of the poufs, where he sat with his head in his hands. When the tea was ready he lifted his head.

Ouma must sit here also. I will have tea and then I will go.

Midhat nodded. Fine. Everyone will take tea. Lili, Raja, Ouma . . . sit. Where's Gabriel?

Where do you think?

Crazy bastard, he muttered. Where is Ouma? Why is everyone here, but her?

She will refuse.

Her husband glanced toward her tent and began to stand up.

Sit, sit. Lili, get her now or there will be problems for all of us.

Ouma's husband glared at Lili until she stood and walked to the tent. She could feel the strength of his eyes following her.

Ouma stood in the middle of the tent. He will kill me, she said.

He wants to have tea.

You don't understand. He must kill me, as a matter of honor. I am sure it was not his idea to come get me. There are others behind this.

He will not kill you. There are no others here and there is no way for you to get out of this. Sit next to me. Sit next to Midhat.

Ouma drew her hood taut about her face and came out of the tent slowly. She sat down next to Lili and her husband began to shift back and forth on his pouf, spilling his tea on Lili's toes.

Careful, Lili said indignantly. Why don't you—

With a great roar, he jumped up, knocked over Lili and snatched Ouma. He held a knife to Ouma's throat. His body shook and rivers of sweat slipped down the side of his face, sliding onto Ouma. Raja backed up, knocked over the kettle and began to cry.

Ouma whimpered. You ran me out of the village, remember? I left and now you want me back. Why?

He started dragging her to the truck without replying. Lili clutched Midhat's sleeve.

How do you expect to get any help with your plan if no one is here to help you?

She could see his mind contemplating her last question. A wicked smile touched his face and he called to Ouma, Are you sure you want me to save you?

She answered with a shriek.

Midhat stayed seated.

You want me to save her? Midhat asked Lili.

She knew she would regret wanting anything from him. Please, she said.

Midhat rummaged through his robes and brought out a gun and waved it in the air. Stop. Unhand that woman, he said and chuckled.

Midhat, he's ignoring you.

Drop her, Midhat shouted.

Shoot it, shoot it. Or give it to me.

Lili reached for the gun, but Midhat held it above his head and stepped back. She stood on her tiptoes and they fought for a moment until Lili wrestled the gun down, lined up the sights, aimed at the sky above their heads and fired. The windshield of the truck splintered into a thousand pieces.

I knew it. Sight is off, said Midhat.

I almost killed them.

Ouma's husband pushed Ouma onto the ground and jumped into his truck.

You will die for this, he shouted out the window.

The engine gunned into action, the wheels spun sand into the air, and the truck headed straight for Ouma. She tore toward the water, ducking behind a palm tree.

He yelled, his face blistering red in the heat, Ouma, you will die and your son will watch.

Ouma's knees gave way. She slipped into the water, beating at it with her fists and cursing her husband until he was long out of sight.

14

Into the Desert

THE ARAB HAD NEVER BROUGHT ME INTO THE DESERT BEFORE. Usually he left me at the hotel in Marrakech or Taroudant with strict instructions to the hotel staff or the watchdog to keep me occupied. It was the work of an old shuwafa—a fortune teller—that prompted him to do it.

We had eaten dinner in one of those old palaces full of tiny blue tiles set into Escher-like patterns and a bronze fountain in the center of the room spouting golden water. The Arab made us sit above the other diners, on a raised platform, his seat a carved teak throne, mine a delicate high-backed chair inlaid with ivory. He had spoken two words to me throughout the dinner, "sit" when we first arrived and I had hovered uncertainly before the platform, and "move" when I blocked his view of the belly dancer.

After dinner, the last dinner of our old life, we found the old hag outside seated behind a stained crate, a worn leather pouf to her side. On the crate were a pack of tarot cards and three cigarettes, the fourth drooped from her mouth, unlit. A scraggly black mustache hung from her upper lip. I tugged on his arm and pointed at the hag. "Don't tell me you believe in this garbage," he said and rolled his eyes.

I determinedly sat down on the pouf. She never looked at the Arab. She stared at me intensely and after several moments of shuffling the cards, she laid out the first one. She eyed me and squinted. She laid out another card and slowly lit the cigarette. She opened her mouth wide and let the smoke drift out, watching the patterns fade away in front of her eyes. With raised eyebrows she said, "Allah has bestowed baraka on you, a great blessing." She put down two more cards. "Do not be anxious about life or death. Help those you can and you may chance upon the one you seek."

She took my hand in hers. Her skin was parched and rough and felt like the hand of a reptile. The Arab growled and pulled me away from her, his fingers pinching blue marks into the flesh of my arm.

At the hotel he made me kneel before him and take him into my mouth. His hands pressed hard against my head and when I struggled, he held me until I gagged.

The next morning, instead of leaving me at the hotel, he took me with him into the desert. I never knew what business the Arab had in the middle of the desert. I didn't know exactly what he did in Caza, Layounne or Marrakech. He had his hand in obscure deals from leather shoes to politics and there was one thing for sure, they all tired me.

I had never seen such a desert, stretching on forever, and it disturbed me. It was hell. We argued about it. The Arab wanted me to get out of the car near the fence in the desert and wait for him to return. "I have business," he said. Of course, I refused. "Five minutes," he said. "No," I said. "Obstinate cunt," he said. "No," I said. "Gypsy bitch," he said, and he reached over me to open the car door. He pushed me onto the ground and spat out, "Gypsy bitch!" at me again. The car door slammed, the motor roared and my face was stung with sand propelled from the tires.

Once he had said gypsy bitch, he didn't have to push me out of the car, I would have left by myself.

15

Watchdog and Russians

THE OASIS HAD BEEN TRANQUIL DURING THE DAY AND THE afternoon wind was beginning to fling sporadic puffs of sand. Lili sat under a tree and picked at the spots of pale pink polish remaining on her nails. The polish color had been inaccurately named Desert Sun. There was nothing pale about the sun in the desert.

An un-desert-like odor trailed before her nostrils. Freshly oiled asphalt. Black smoke suspended along the windless streets. The coagulated smell of city gutters after rain.

She turned around and a man stood a short distance away, surveying the oasis with slitted eyes. He was one of the ugliest men she had ever seen, with a great hooked nose and a flat cruel forehead. His face was matted with thick scars that ran along his cheekbones and discolored his dark skin. Her body went cold—the Arab's watchdog. The Arab had sent him to collect her.

He planted his feet and bellowed out, Isn't there anyone here?

What he meant was, aren't there any men here? Heat flooded back into her body, he didn't know who she was. She was just another woman from the desert. She scurried toward her tent, hunched over so that her robe covered her feet, her sandals being the only recognizable piece of her that was visible. She was relieved to be wearing her robe, although she was surprised he didn't recognize it, there

77

wasn't a finer one in Morocco and he was with the Arab and her when they had ordered it from the tailor.

Inside the tent, she peeped through a crack to see him still standing in the same place, hands on hips, cruel brow furrowed. Midhat appeared from his tent, limping.

Shalom, he said. What can I do for you?

I am looking for a man.

Lili's breath came out in harsh gasps and she had a difficult time hearing their conversation. Her hands trembled so hard that she couldn't control them.

We see many men here, said Midhat.

You know who I am looking for.

The watchdog stared at Midhat's foot. Midhat stood straighter and balanced on both feet. The watchdog stepped toward him.

Can you describe him? he asked tentatively.

The watchdog sneered. Would you really like me to describe him . . . *Midhat?*

Midhat blinked. No, no. That will not be necessary.

Good. Also, he may have had a girl with him. White hair, skin like fine desert sand. We are looking for her.

Lili's body erupted in sweat. She ran to the cracked mirror and looked at herself. Her eyes were beady and shallow without their usual coating of mascara, liner and shadow. The color of her skin was dark now, not as dark as a Berber, more like mud at the bottom of the water. She pushed back the hood to see that the roots of her hair were growing out to a flat brown. No wonder the watchdog hadn't recognized her.

No, Midhat said. No girl with white hair and skin such as that.

Midhat knew the Arab. Did he really not know the watchdog was looking for her or was he saving her again?

The watchdog folded his arms and gazed around the oasis, at the various tents, at the lunatic in the bushes with the goats, at the fierce desert all around.

When did you see him last?

He never arrived. No, he never arrived.

I am sure they were here.

I said he didn't arrive.

I say he did.

No. Why would I lie to you?

The watchdog stepped close to Midhat, Lili saw the shine of a knife. In one movement, he stepped on Midhat's injured foot and held the tip of the knife to Midhat's ear, slowly moving the blade. Midhat's turban tilted crazily, a line of blood appeared down his neck. Lili knew the watchdog also carried a gun. Surely Midhat would turn her in. She was ready to flee out the back of the tent.

You tell me *first* if you see them, not the police.

The watchdog stepped back and walked away, leaving Midhat in the center of the tents, standing with a dark drop of blood running down his neck. His gaze was peaceful. Slowly, a triumphant grin spread between his cheeks.

Midhat adjusted his turban and limped straight to Lili's tent, speaking as he walked. There was a man here looking for you, he called.

Lili wanted to hide in the dark shadows of the tent and not answer. She wanted to go back in time, back to her old life of anesthetized nights and rubber conversations. Or bury herself in the sand or crawl between the blankets and flatten herself into nonexistence. What was the point? He knew she was inside.

Who? she asked through the wall.

He was a nice-looking man. Rich.

No he wasn't.

Rich enough to give me money for you. Maybe I ought to call him back.

She would have to find her savior and leave the oasis as soon as possible. If she didn't, either the watchdog would discover her, the Arab would get her or Midhat would turn her in. She stepped outside the tent. She stared at the blood dripping down Midhat's neck.

What do you want?

Nothing. He smiled his wide false grin.

Shortly before sunset, Midhat gathered them around him. He jostled from foot to foot, robes swishing, forgetting all about his missing toes. He pointed excitedly at a dust cloud moving in their direction. In the midst of the dust were several men, who were riding their mules spread-legged, instead of sideways like the desert people.

Midhat whispered proudly, Here they are. These are the Russians. The Russians are coming.

The Russians were coming. Lili felt her blood move faster, here was her chance to escape. She would approach them, tell them she was one of them and give them the gold chains as payment to take her back with them. They would embrace her as one of them. Luck was throwing a plan into her path and soon she would be gone.

Why are you whispering? asked Lili.

Quiet.

Don't they know they are Russians?

They are the best at spying. They say they can read your words merely by looking at your lips.

Then, Ouma said, they will read your whispers.

Shh. I don't want them to suspect anything.

Suspect what?

Anything.

They stared at the three men approaching. Certainly, the men were taller than any of them, with the exception of Lili, with thick faces and a heavy way of moving their hands. The men were not Arabs or Berbers, maybe they were Russians.

I want to hear them speak, said Lili.

I've brought them here to show you they exist, not for tea and a chat.

I want to talk to them.

Are you crazy? You can't talk to them, said Midhat, edging toward the Russians protectively. Stay away from these men. They are not to be trifled with. Mad and dangerous.

He walked away flapping his arms as if to shoo her away from them. Lili didn't care what Midhat said, they were her countrymen and they couldn't possibly be as mad as he was. They were her saviors.

Gabriel leaned toward her, bouncing energetically on his tiptoes to be nearer to her ear. He looked around and tugged at the loose threads dangling from his frayed cuff. His hands were disproportionately large for his delicate wrist bones.

I must warn you, he said in a low voice. Be careful of Ouma. She is the one who is dangerous.

Yes, she is.

No, you must listen. She is one of them.

Who?

The disappeared.

Lili looked across the campsite at Ouma. But she is here.

He sighed. The dunes can hide anything. They are deceptive and must be watched closely, if you want to know them. He leaned closer to Lili and said, She was released. She was one of the disappeared and now she has been released. By the gov . . . ern . . . ment. He drew the word out in three slow syllables.

Imprisoned? You're saying Ouma is a rebel? Anyway, she's not interested in politics.

That is not one of the requirements of the disappeared.

What are the requirements?

Gabriel waved his hand dismissively and tugged at the strings unraveling from his elbows, widening the hole by several inches. I am in trouble, he said.

What have you done?

Done? I've done nothing. It is she who has done to me.

Who?

Someone who keeps the heat of the desert away with her coolness. Yet in one glance, she makes sweat pour down my body. Do you understand?

Oh, well, Lili smiled flirtatiously.

Of course, she thought, it was Gabriel who had touched her. He was surprisingly poetic with his words. She eyed his tiny frame and tried to imagine it in the same positions as the Arab. Somehow his smallness got in the way.

I am cursed, he said.

It is not a problem, there is no trouble. Maybe with time she will return your feelings. You never know.

She already does.

Lili frowned at his presumptuousness.

But that is not the problem, it is all so impossible. He gave Lili a meaningful look as he walked off. There will be trouble. Big trouble.

Lili lay motionless in her bed until she heard the heavy breathing of Ouma's night sleep. She tiptoed out of the tent and headed toward the Russians' camp. She would tell them everything. She clutched at the pouch around her neck and took each step slowly and stealthily.

A tangle of clouds hung in front of the burnished moon. Sand swirled across the desert floor like smoke. Perfect to cover her footprints. First she slipped by Midhat's tent, which was dark, then past Fatima and Raja's. The wind threw grains of sand against the walls, whispering in her ears.

Lili, Lili.

She ignored the harsh whispers. It was the blood in her ears and sand on the walls. She could see a flickering light in Fatima's tent and hoped both of them were inside. Ahead of her, farther into the desert, the Russians were sitting around a small fire.

Lili, Lili, the wind whispered. And then coughed.

Lili froze. The Arab. She crouched down to the ground and rolled herself up into a tight ball, clutching her head between her knees, waiting to be killed.

Lili, Lili.

Lili's breath choked inside her.

Lili, it's me, Fatima. Come to me, please.

It wasn't the Arab, only Fatima. The blood in her ears quieted down to a low pulse. She wouldn't stop for Fatima. How did Fatima know it was her anyway? She continued on.

Lili, Lili.

Her voice reverberated in the quiet of the night. Fatima scared Lili.

Lili, Fatima's voice grew louder and shriller. Lili.

Even in bright daylight her tent looked frightening. Big and weather scarred with aged stains and every tear repaired with bold stitches to perfection. It reminded Lili more of a cave than a tent. She turned and went back to the tent and hesitated before the doorway.

Quiet, she whispered to Fatima. How did you know it was me?

I know many things now that I am blind.

Why are you calling my name?

Lili stepped inside. A candle flickered in one corner. In the opposite corner, in a place of honor, was a medium-sized television set complete with a rabbit-ears antenna. It looked as if you could walk over and switch it on.

Lili had had a television one time. The Arab brought one to her apartment, to keep her company, he said. He turned it on before he left and she had watched it until he returned. English nature programs, Arabic game shows, French cooking, Spanish sitcoms. She slept in front of the flickering light. Three days later when the Arab walked in, she was still there, hair unwashed, body unkempt. He threw the television out the window. Broken glass, shrieks from the neighbors. Don't you have any self-control? he had hollered at her. The problem was, she had too much.

Fatima lay stretched out on her bed. The other, Raja's, lay empty.

I cannot sleep with Raja in the tent, Fatima said. Not after she tried to murder me.

It was not you she was trying to murder. Besides, Raja is not here.

She sticks me with my pins all night long. As soon as I am asleep, she stabs me with one and then pretends she is asleep. You have cursed this oasis.

This oasis had bad luck long before I arrived.

There is no such thing as luck, it is all the will of Allah. Fatima covered her face with her hands. The dark frightens me.

Isn't everything dark?

Night is a different dark.

What does it matter? What does morning bring that the night doesn't?

I see more now that I am blind.

Lili frowned and stood directly over Fatima. She held the candle over Fatima's head and slowly tilted it as if she were going to pour wax over her. Fatima's face was drawn into hundreds of little wrinkles, not in a squint, but as if her face were drawing inward to escape the night.

I know who you are and why you are here.

Lili's hand shook a drop of wax onto Fatima's blanket.

She sat down on a springy benchlike couch with several stiff camel skins thrown over the back. An elaborate woven rug ran along the length of it. It was the only real piece of furniture Lili had seen at the oasis.

Midhat has brought her here to dishonor us.

Her? Lili asked.

And then he will marry the whore.

Who?

You. It is his way, I know.

Lili stood to go.

Don't leave.

I'm leaving.

Help me. Raja hides things, Fatima said. When I try to find them, they are gone. You have to look.

I can't pry.

You're not. This is my tent. She cannot hide her things from me, no secrets, she is only darra, the second wife. Look under there. What do you see? She pointed to a floor cushion.

Lili lifted it. Nothing.

Underneath the cushion, it was true there was nothing. Under the rug, she saw something. She glanced at Fatima staring at the ceiling. Silently, delicately, she pulled up the rug to reveal several pieces of torn paper. She slid them out. The first few were blank, but then she gaped in amazement—they were drawings, charcoal sketches in incredible detail. At first the subject was not obvious, merely because she couldn't believe what she was seeing. Any way she turned them, they were the same. Men's penises.

I hear you. What have you found?

Lili couldn't reply.

They were anatomically correct and not only that, each was of a different man. It was quite obvious. One was even uncircumcised and Lili knew it was forbidden for a Muslim woman to have sex with an uncircumcised man, let alone a man not her husband.

It is nothing. Pieces of paper bags. Old shopping bags.

Yes, she covets these things. Western clothes and shoes.

That's all. Where is Raja?

That is another one of her secrets.

Lili carefully put the drawings back and stood to leave.

I'm leaving. Goodnight.

There is no good night.

Lili made her way to the Russians' camp and stopped in the shadows. Against the firelight, Lili studied their silhouettes. Two men sat at the fire talking in low voices. One with a shock of hair and the other with no hair. The bald one stood up and kicked sand at a tent.

Get her out of here. She's probably a spy.

Someone came out of one of the tents and hesitated in the dim light, pulling the hood of his robe tight to his face. Someone short with a round body. Lili was sure it was Raja. But why would Raja go to the Russians? Midhat would immediately return her to her family if he knew.

The third Russian, with short silver hair that glittered in the firelight, also came out of the tent and stood with his arms folded. He was tall, made taller by the leaping flames.

A spy? You have been reading too many Russian novels. He laughed, his deep voice beating back the dark night.

Someone grabbed Lili from behind and placed a hand over her mouth, then moved his other hand to her neck.

Do not scream. I will slowly take my hand away.

Lili turned to see Midhat. Midhat. She had to get him away from here or he would see Raja.

What are you doing here? he demanded.

I . . . the Russians—

Forget the Russians. I told you before. You can talk to them in the morning.

Why are they here? Lili asked.

They are dangerous. Now go.

Yes.

Well, go then. Leave.

Lili didn't move.

Fool girl. Midhat grabbed her arm. Stay away or I will have to kill you. Your life is mine now.

He pulled her back to her tent and thrust her inside, slowly walking backward to make sure she did not leave again. Lili stayed awake until she saw the soft shadow of Raja returning to her tent.

16

Second Death

I WAS TWELVE YEARS OLD THE SECOND TIME I DIED. EVERY DETAIL of that journey along the Bosphorus is still fixed in my mind.

The evening was so calm I could hear twinklings of music from the Istanbul shore, an accordion that reminded me of Russia. The ship, named *Nedezda*, cut straight through the center of the strait. Boats, so many boats, crisscrossed around, at all angles, buzzing like flies. Istanbul was a chaotic city with houses crawling up the hills and palaces built on water. People lived in those honeycomb houses, crowded next to each other as if there were no land left in the world. Mosques lay among its hills, squat beetles pinpointed with minarets stabbing at the sky like antennas.

Far down the river, way in front of the boat was a little white tower set out from the land, surrounded by water. It had made me intensely sad, it looked so lonely.

To my right passed a party boat with men dressed in black and the women brighter than spring blooms in their lovely colors. A few of the men turned and gazed at the big ship, then turned back to the party without acknowledging me high up on my perch. The deck of their boat was green and the tables were covered in white cloths.

One woman in a pure yellow dress had stood on the tip-top deck, her hair whipping behind, her face flung into the wind and arms stretched open to her sides. The lines of her slim body showed through the dress, the length of her legs, the roundness of her stomach. A radiant smile blossomed across her face.

A man stood behind her, he put a hand on her shoulder for it seemed the woman would take flight and float over the sea.

Years later I had asked the Arab for a yellow dress and he had returned with the shimmery gold one, not the real, pure yellow I had explained in detail to him.

"Nobody wears yellow," he had said. Put it on. If I had liked him even a little I might have told him about the woman in yellow.

By the time the ship had made its way through the Bosphorus, evening had fallen. Prayer calls wailed across the water, echoing from all sides. Lights along the waterfront began to glow. On my right I saw a giant mosque, grander than any of the others, with minarets that illuminated with rows of yellow dots. It changed from a great round beetle to a grand castle, reaching up to the night sky.

As the boat passed the lonely little tower, it turned into a gaily lit spectacle with a tiny, perfect red light blinking in front of it. I leaned toward the beckoning light and tumbled headfirst into the icy water of the Bosphorus.

17

Ouma's Village

Someone was inside Lili's tent with her, sobbing in a low methodical way that went on and on, in a flat tone. The sound was coming from the corner farthest from Lili and Ouma's beds and although the sky outside had lightened considerably in the early morning, Lili could not discern a shape in the darkness of the tent. Ouma lay bundled in her bed, oblivious to the noise.

Who is it? Lili whispered.

The sound continued.

Stop it.

On and on the sound went, filling the little tent with its sadness.

Ouma? Psst, do you hear that?

There was no reply, so Lili slid out of her bed and tiptoed over to Ouma. She tapped Ouma to awaken her and found a crumpled blanket. Her bed was empty. Lili ran to the door flap and opened it to let in some light. A small heap lay shaking in the corner, cowering beneath a blanket.

Lili gently lifted the blanket and found Ouma sobbing with her eyes wide open. Lili crouched in front of her. Ouma looked straight at Lili, but there was no recognition and she continued with her rhythmic crying. The tattoo on her forehead was black against the whiteness of her skin and it scared Lili. She covered Ouma with the blanket again and considered what to do. The sobbing dominated her mind, she walked in tiny circles trying to think. Lili felt like crying. No crying, no crying, she reminded herself. Lili's eyes stung, she gave a loud sniff and with that Ouma gasped, crumpling onto the floor.

Ouma, Lili unwrapped her from the blanket. Ouma?

Ouma slowly opened her eyes. Fat tears spilled down her face. She focused on the room and gazed at Lili for several moments. Her hand wiped the tears from her face and she looked at the wetness on her fingertips with surprise.

I was crying.

Yes.

Such a sad dream.

It's all right, the dream is gone.

The dream is not gone. My son . . . I must see him.

When?

Now. Do you remember when we first met? It is time now, you must come with me and help me.

Now? It is too dangerous, your husband will kill you.

I need to see him. Surely you understand?

We have to plan this. And first there are the Russians. I will talk to them this morning.

The Russians are gone.

Gone? What do you mean gone?

Lili ran out of her tent without her robe, turned around, rushed back in, put her robe on and dashed out again. The vestiges of night were still in the sky and several stars outshone the sun. The Russians' tents were gone.

They left early this morning, Ouma said. Before light. With Midhat.

Bastard. I can't believe it. He said they would be here today. He hurried those Russians away. Bastard.

Why should you care about the Russians?

Do you know where they went?

I will go to see my son and you must come with me. Just to look at him. Then we will find your Russians.

Lili turned in a circle, searching the empty desert. The pale sky extended until it engulfed all below. The oasis felt small and contained . . . safe. Was she becoming agoraphobic? Afraid to leave her little universe? She desperately wanted to leave the oasis, but only with protection and someone to hide her. What if the watchdog were out there waiting? Or the police? It all depended on the Russians. They could offer her the safety and the escape. She would find them. She pulled her hood over her head.

How will we find them? They could be anywhere.

Russians cannot disappear in the desert.

Ouma and Lili stood before the camels. The beasts lay underneath a cluster of trees, shifting and grunting, suspiciously eyeing the women out of the corner of their huge eyes. The lunatic approached them through the thorny bushes and Ouma waved him away, stomping her foot and flailing her arms. He looked surprised and retreated, hovering across the water from them.

We can take the fast ones, Ouma said. We will be there in two hours.

Lili had never been on a camel before. The bony arched backs looked horribly uncomfortable. And none of the camels looked very fast.

They are Midhat's. And they seem unfriendly.

We need to hurry. Ouma pointed to one of the camels. Take this one. This is a nice one.

Lili looked at the camel. It refused to meet her stare. Despite the ridiculous tuft of toupee-like hair between its ears, it looked alarmingly evil when it drew its lips back in a grimace.

I don't like this, she said. What if Midhat catches us?

So what? Ouma laughed shrilly. What's he going to do, kill you? Beat me? Stone me? He'll have to get in line for that.

The sun was so hot it was loud, only coolness could bring quiet to Lili's throbbing ears. Ouma unfurled a long, long scarf and wrapped it

around and around Lili, covering her face, ears and neck. The camel
stood up and gurgled. It was tall. Lili looked at its feet. They were
big, round and padded, swollen looking. Soft and squishy. A hundred
times the size of a cat's foot without the nails.

Ouma held up a small V-shaped piece of leather. Do you see, special saddles? It will be easy.

She made a strange *shhh-shhh* noise and the camel bowed, its front
legs doubling over until it touched the ground. Then its hind legs
creaked and collapsed in a double-jointed bend. Ouma threw the saddle up onto the camel's back, tightened a few things and motioned for
Lili to throw her leg over.

Lili sidled up to the camel. The creature craned its neck around to
look at her through its glistening bulb-eyes, giving her a long-lashed
wink. She lifted her leg over the saddle and the camel roared. Lili
froze, leg suspended in the air. Ouma pushed her onto the saddle and
the camel rose up, up and up into the air. Lili felt precariously balanced
and clutched the saddle horn with both hands, her knuckles white.

Relax, Ouma instructed her. Relax.

The camels walked calmly, taking great strides across the sand. Lili
clenched her eyes shut so she would not have to look at the vast
desert in front of her. As the oasis drew farther away, she felt vulnerable, only two things existed in the desert: sand and sky, and they
had faded to one brilliant shade of white. No other colors or dimen-
sions. Lili knew it was the shadows she had to watch for, the folds
and crevices. A shadow could hide anything. She opened her eyes.
She was a long way up. Sand and gravel and more sand.

The sun crushed them, the only movement of air came from the
camels lashing her back and forth in a movement a bit like Latin
dancing. Or sex.

She thought of the little green bird struggling across the desert inferno. She felt its exhaustion, its heart pounding, its parched throat,
the brilliant feathers growing dull in the intense sunlight. The vision
of an oasis, was it real or a mirage? The last few wing strokes before it

reached the water, only to plunge out of the sky. Lili jolted awake as she felt herself falling out of the sky. She latched on to the camel's mane and pulled herself upright. The camel curved its neck around and gave her a look of annoyance.

She concentrated on the terrain. For the first hour nothing changed, then suddenly there were stones and desiccated bushes and a bleached Pepsi can. An outcropping of rocks appeared in front of them, huddled like nomads on the horizon.

As they neared the outcropping, the rocks transformed into a red-walled sandstone village that blended into the barren eroded hills, until nothing except the squared walls and blunt roofs separated the village from the earth itself. Lili had the impression that with one good rainfall the village would melt completely into the ground, villagers, trees and walls all a flat red mud.

They stopped the camels outside the village, where two dusty men crouched listlessly in the shade of a group of sand-swept date palms.

Here is where we can leave the camels, Ouma said, as she drew the hood of her djellaba tight about her face. You talk to them, this is my village.

One of the men approached her, a red-skinned, one-eyed man who blended in with the dirt. He took the camel and Ouma and Lili walked toward an entrance in the wall. The air in the village pushed tight and dense around them after the wide freedom of the desert.

And there were people everywhere. They moved and shuffled so fast, Lili felt bewildered. She hadn't seen so many people since Casablanca and that seemed ages ago. Her head stuck up far above the villagers, who were much shorter than the people in the city. She rounded her shoulders and withdrew into her robe.

The village has gone crazy, Ouma mumbled from her hood.

She stopped in the middle of the street and turned to Lili. She grabbed on to Lili's arms with strong fingers and hissed, Today is Âid al Kabir. Look.

Lili looked around. The shops were closed, people talked in excited voices, laughing and smiling. Men milled about the streets, while women hurried along the narrow alleys, loaves of bread clutched under their arms, robes fluttering about their feet. Children played in doorways, where the bleating lambs were tied, adding to the cacophony of noise.

Slaughter of lambs.

Allah have mercy. Now we will have to go directly to the house to see my son.

Ouma, you cannot.

Ouma turned and gave Lili a furtive glance before starting through the crowds, one hand held out in front of her to clear the way, the other clutching her robe tight around her neck. Lili could see her, moving ahead, zigzagging through the crowds. Lili tried to walk faster. People jostled her in different directions and Ouma's bobbing head moved farther away.

Ouma, she called, Ouma, and then she slapped a hand over her mouth. What was she thinking? Calling out her name would put Ouma in danger.

The entire population had emptied into the streets, shouting to each other, hawking bright tangerines and striped melons, burning spicy incense.

The sun had lowered in the sky and shadows grew in the narrow streets. Ouma was gone. As she neared the center of the town, a man called out, *Allah Akbar*. The man stood above the crowd in the semi-darkness of his doorway. His black eyes searched the crowd until they found Lili, sinking far into her, holding her captive, until he called out again and in one quick movement brought a gleaming knife across the throat of the ram he held.

Blood so red she didn't know such a red existed, spotted the white-washed doorway. The ram twitched and jumped and slumped. Blood kept flowing down the steps, along the street, making its way toward her, to her feet, to the insides of her thighs and straight into her center.

She screamed and ran into an alley and up a flight of narrow stairs. She kept running and climbing and stumbling, astonished faces peering from windows, a beating of drums now adding to her panic—the slaughter began, the streets slick with blood, her shoes drenched with the red of it all.

Finally in front of her, a ladder led up. She jumped on it and climbed to the top, where she found a wide white roof decorated with flapping laundry. Below her was the city displayed in a pattern of mazes. She saw the alleys she had run through, the steps she had climbed. The city ran with blood, slick cobblestones, speckled walls, splattered melons.

Behind her she found footprints of blood. She took off her shoe and her toenails were lined in bright crimson. The hem of her robe left streaks along the sides of the footprints.

She took a deep breath, she inhaled the iron-metal smell of blood mixed with the powdery odor of the hot clay city walls. She looked out at the city again. The camels were closer than she thought. A man stood on a rooftop, several rooftops away. She heard a noise and turned quickly—it was only laundry flapping.

The man watched her, arms folded, chin up. He stood with his legs apart, one toe tapping. It was the Arab. He did not react when she recognized him. Her legs gave way and she sat down on the roof. He found her and now he would kill her. How could she ever think a snake so small could kill him? Small whimpers escaped from her every time she exhaled. A figure appeared behind him and he turned and smiled.

As soon as he smiled, she knew it was not the Arab, not the slightest bit like him. She must have been crazy to think so. She stood up on her weak legs.

The Arab. If he hadn't been bitten by that stupid snake, she wouldn't be here in the middle of the desert at a barbaric slaughter. She would be back in Caza, gold gown intact, cold gin-and-tonic in her hand, dressing for the night. Or waking in the morning to the smell of imported coffee and flowers, luxuriating in her morning bath before heading off for a manicure. She looked at her nails. Horrid. It was a good thing the Arab was dead. If there was one thing he was adamant about, it was grooming. He could smell as vile as a garbage heap, but she had better have clean nails and smell like a rose.

Over on the rooftop, the couple embraced. A rage built inside her. Rage at being in this predicament, rage at the Arab for leaving her in the desert, rage at the village for all the blood and most of all, rage at the couple for embracing.

She heard a noise again and turned quickly. Again the rooftop was empty, except for the gentle flapping of the laundry. Was that a dark shape she saw behind the gray sheets?

She listened carefully, there was only the incessant buzzing of the flies. The sound filled her ears and she knew she must find Ouma. There was something bad about this town. Was it possible she did not know how to act in a town anymore, that she had become unsocialized?

She whirled abruptly and ran into a hard surface, a person with the hood of a djellaba over his eyes. A shadow encased his face hiding his expression and features. He held her in a strong grip and brought his face close to hers. His beard tickled her. She felt the shape of his lips press onto hers—long, not short and bowed like Midhat's. Long and strong. Then he was kissing her and she pushed and pushed him away, but his grip pulled her in and his lips were so gentle she was forced to be still.

This was a kiss. Light, fearful yet tense with delight. His lips hovered over hers, barely touching, pressing with a dampness that wasn't wet.

She twisted her torso and he stumbled. With one great heave, she shoved him over the roof. As much as she may have enjoyed it, she did not give him permission to put his lips on hers. He landed on the street below. She watched until she saw him push himself onto his hands and knees and she ran for the ladder.

The streets flew by her in reverse order, the kiss blotting out the stench and the brilliance of the blood now mixed with dull dirt, dark against the cobbled bricks.

18

Lili

I ARRIVED IN TANGIERS, AT MADAME MER'S DOOR, UNCONSCIOUS and shaking with fever from the oily waters of the Bosphorus. I later heard she had tried to force the ship captain to take me back with him. He refused and she threw one of her pointy-toed shoes at him in an unladylike way that made the girls whisper malicious tales behind her back. It also gave me an unfair reputation as a troublemaker before I was even aware that I had been reborn as Lili.

The day I opened my eyes, Madame Mer looked at me with her squinty gaze, walked in a slow circle around me and declared, "You will be Lili. You will have blond hair and the nature of a . . ." She gazed around the room and found nothing, so that when she saw a bird hoping about on the windowsill, she said, ". . . bird. You will sing."

Later, the maid told me that the bird was a black-bellied plover, not known for its note-carrying ability.

Rosa said, "You're lucky. The day I arrived, the cook came back from the market with a basketful of cod and she told me I was to swim with the calm nature of a fish."

Each of us had her own forte. The water-stained copy of Degas' ballerinas hanging above the sink launched half a dozen girls into ballet and painting. A week's supply of potatoes on the counter, a chef. The mundane whistling of a street child, a flutist.

We should have hated our forced talents. Instead, we took to them as if our lives depended on them. Singing transported me into a different world, where I wasn't tall and there was no Arab or Madame Mer. Rosa was a true fish in the water, swimming effortlessly, and she dove beautifully. Poor Rosa, she had been a charming child, but grew into an unsightly young woman. Her upper lip and nose protruded, her chin retreated and her hair hung limp as strings. She became the fish that Madame Mer requested.

Maybe the Buddhists have it right. Until I reach Nirvana, I'm stuck in a cycle of reincarnation and with each new life I'm given a new name and my old name is wiped from my memory. So, at some point, when I die my third death, Lili will disappear and I will be given a new name.

19

After the Kiss

LILI RAN AROUND CORNERS AND MORE CORNERS, THE PRESSURE of the lips urging her on, her eyes guiding her way through the streets as she ran, her mind only seeing the kiss. A blur of red walls, shiny cobblestones, dark faces until she came upon Ouma crouched across from a house and hidden behind a donkey cart. She wondered if Ouma would be able to tell.

She touched Ouma on the shoulder. Ouma turned quickly and grabbed her by the throat. Her eyes stared into Lili's with a force Lili had never seen before.

It's me, it's me. Lili stepped back and Ouma released her. What is wrong with you? What is wrong with this town?

Ouma didn't reply, she went back to her vigil. Lili inspected the house Ouma was watching. In front hung a clothesline draped with rags stained rusty red. A girl sat on a low stool holding a yellow flower in her fist. With the other hand, she plucked off the petals one by one, placing them in her palm and blowing on them gently until they slipped off her hand.

Through the window, Lili saw a man. He moved past the window, gesturing with a closed fist. It was not Ouma's husband, it was the bald Russian. Another head appeared in the window—the silver-haired Russian.

Lili crouched beside Ouma. She could hear fragments of sentences:
We find them . . . Midhat sell us . . .

What? Ouma, what did they say about Midhat?

Ouma turned and looked at Lili wide-eyed. I can't understand a
word they say.

What?

Lili listened again and watched the girl tear off another petal. It
drifted this way and that, twisting and careening in the air until
it landed in a puddle of blood that lay at the girl's feet. She could hear
snatches of sentences from the house.

Good . . . buy legs . . .

They are talking about Midhat selling them something. Good legs.
Did you hear that?

Lili, I cannot understand them.

He must be selling women to the Russians.

The bastard. I know he will sell just about anyone anything, but
women—that has gone too far. What language are they speaking? I
don't know this language.

Lili looked at her, surprised. I . . . I'm not sure.

Well, I think it's Russian.

Russian?

Of course. Lili smiled, they were speaking her own native tongue.
After ten years, she was hearing Russian. And she still understood
some of it. She felt a burst of affection, a camaraderie, with the Russians. Her people. She belonged to them.

I will go talk to them, Lili said.

She stood up and started for the house, pulling her hood off with a
flourish, a great grin across her face. Something hard hit her from behind. She fell down flat on the ground and found herself staring at a
trampled cigarette butt. The little girl with the yellow flower ran off.
Close to her arm was the pool of blood strewn with yellow petals that
floated like little boats in a cerise lake. A few of them had become
saturated and the yellow had turned orange.

Then someone wearing a hooded djellaba heaved her up and
pulled her down an alley.

Fool, the person hissed. The hood fell back to reveal Midhat. You are ruining everything.

Midhat.

What are you doing here? he asked. And where is that little witch? I know she is here with you.

Who?

Who? He raised his fist as if to strike her. Who? Ouma, that's who. Where is she?

Lili looked cautiously around. No sign of Ouma.

She is not here.

She must be here or you wouldn't be here. How did you get here? How did you find me?

I wasn't looking for you.

He narrowed his eyes and his round lips tensed into a straight line. Foam formed in the corners of his mouth. Tell me what you are doing here.

I was going to talk to the Russians.

No! You cannot talk to them.

You told me they would be at the oasis in the morning and I could talk to them.

They will come to the oasis a second time. That is part of my plan. Now leave.

You are lying to me. I want to talk to them now.

No. Now leave or I will kill you. I won't let a little whore get in the way of my plan.

You won't kill me, you need me for your plan.

Need you or not, you are too much trouble. His hand moved to his knife. Are you going to be a good girl? Let me see you run. Run!

Lili turned and stalked off. This was the most nonsensical town she had ever been to. It made the oasis seem normal.

Back at the camel park, Lili found that Ouma had already taken her camel and left. Far off in the distance, Lili could see a figure on a camel.

When did she leave? Lili demanded of the old one-eyed man.

He would not look at her, only pointed vaguely into the desert. Lili leaned down and put her face next to the old man's. His watery eye flicked back and forth before making contact with one of hers and resting there as if it were weary.

Tell me, is that her? Lili pointed to the figure.

He squinted into the desert and nodded an affirmation.

By the time the camel was saddled and Lili sat astride, the figure had almost disappeared from the horizon.

Going out of town, toward its home, Lili's camel jogged along at a good speed. The figure on the horizon quickly drew closer and soon they were approaching Ouma.

Ouma, Lili called.

Lili's camel kept going straight past the other camel, not slowing down, going faster if anything. She pulled hard on her reins. The camel ignored her and continued on. Lili turned around and looked at Ouma huddled deep into her djellaba. It wasn't Ouma. Lili's camel stuck its neck out, brayed with all its strength and with a great lurch took off.

Gabriel? Lili called.

She was sure it had been Gabriel on the camel. She had seen foreign shoes sticking out from under the robe. Lili twisted around for a quick glimpse to see that the person sat hunched over, not a speck of the face showing. Far in front of her, a second camel answered hers with an equally loud bray and her camel shifted into full gallop.

Lili held on with both hands and tried to relax. She was on her way toward the second camel, like it or not. The joggling of the camel loosened something in her brain and a revelation popped into her head—it was not legs that the Russians had said that Midhat was selling them, it was arms. Midhat was selling arms to the Russians. She was near the second camel now and she recognized the robe Ouma had been wearing.

Ouma, she called out, Ouma. It's not legs, it's arms.

The figure turned. It was Ouma.

The Russians are not buying legs, they are buying arms. I translated it wrong. Arms, not legs. It was the wrong word.

Arms? Ouma said. Arms?

Yes, I'm certain.

Ouma stared ahead, her expression sharpened. Maybe you are right.

I am?

I think I understand now. Midhat, that bastard. He is a devious man. Devious.

What do you understand?

I understand what is happening. You have helped me as I said you would. You have cleared my mind.

What is happening? Why were you spying on the Russians? Did you see your son?

I was not spying on the Russians.

All right, why were you watching the Russians?

I was not watching the Russians. I thought someone else might be there.

I was afraid your husband would see you.

It is not my husband I am afraid of.

Midhat was looking for you.

Oh?

You must have seen him.

No. Did he see me?

No. Gabriel did.

Gabriel?

That was Gabriel behind us.

Where?

Look.

They turned around and searched the desert. No one was there.

He was there. I saw him. He was following behind you. If you weren't watching the Russians, were you looking for your son?

He lives without me. Ouma sighed and gazed off into the distance. I was looking for my lover.

Your lover would have been with the Russians?

Never. He hated the Russians. It is the Russians I fear and so should you. Promise me you will have nothing to do with them.

Ouma, I don't understand.

Promise me.

Yes, okay.

He should have come to see me. My lover is late.

I wouldn't worry, he will come.

This is the problem. There is something wrong and it is Midhat. Midhat is dealing with the Russians and my lover never would have. He wouldn't.

Midhat knew your lover?

Oh Lili, you cannot know these things. You are here to help, not to know.

20

Escape

ONE DAY I LOST THE WATCHDOG IN THE JEWELRY SOUK. THE MARKET was crammed with stalls selling carved wooden spoons, cotton sports socks, painted silk and ragged fennec furs.

We were wandering through the narrow alleys and I stopped at a table laden with gold and silver. There was a Berber necklace made of silver and red coral. I handed it to the owner and told him I wanted to buy it. The watchdog handed me some money and stood outside the stall, hands deep in his pockets, leering at all the women shopping. I casually walked into the depths of the stall and—it was easy—I walked out the back door and left him standing in the front. Poor shopkeeper.

I headed straight for the center: Djemaa El Fna. The Arab had told me it was dangerous and a woman like me shouldn't want to go there. Dangerous or not, the place attracted me. I had heard too many tales of the music and storytellers and acrobats and snake charmers.

The square was crowded. I knew it was always crowded. The turmoil of it all.

A woman dressed from head to toe in a thin black-and-orange animal print djellaba offered henna designs for feet and hands. Her gauze veil covered nothing. A provocative, fuck-you djellaba.

The water boys were there, twirling their hats with slight movements of their necks. Storytellers, men dressed in women's clothing, tatty stuffed bras over their shirts, acted out their tales. Snake charmers, with their vipers' mouths stitched shut, blew on their pipes. Acrobats wearing red rags bounced off the asphalt in their bare feet.

Then for the most daring event of the afternoon, I went to the Café de France for a mint tea. Me, by myself. This had never happened.

The chaotic square spread in front of me. A breeze blew the steam off my tea. The glass boys arrived. Two of them rode up on a dilapidated scooter, a stretch-skin drum dangling off the shoulders of the man on the back. The driver spread out a grayed and torn towel, the other unloaded a basket of green bottles. The man with the drum began to pound a beat. The other shattered the green bottles one by one on the ground, the tinkling sound wafting over to where I sat.

When he finished, he sat on the gray towel and slowly, slowly lowered his back onto the shards, rocking back and forth. After a few moments, he bounced up and turned in a slow circle, his back and shoulders glittering with red drops and a gash that produced one fat drop of blood. He approached a bespectacled man and made him come forward and hold out his hands. He dumped a handful of the glass into the man's hands. The man stepped back and gingerly released the glass. The glass man knelt and crushed the glass in his hands as if he were kneading bread.

I thought about how nice it would be to smash a basket of green bottles on the asphalt.

A throat cleared next to me and a rumbling voice asked, "May I sit here?"

In English. With a real accent. American or Canadian. A buzz ran through my stomach at the sound of such a voice. Land of the free, home of the brave. Was it possible to fall in love with an accent?

"All the tables are taken," he said.

"Of course," I answered.

"Thanks."

I stared at his arms. He had lots of little blond hairs on them. When he spoke to the waiter, I looked at him. His eyebrows were dark and the hair on his head was the same color as the hair on his arms. Real blond hair. Mine was fake and I was embarrassed by it until I remembered he couldn't see it under the hood of my djellaba.

While he was ordering from the waiter, I picked up my tea and at the same time, his plastic lighter that lay next to his cigarettes. I slipped it under my robe to look at the writing on it: "Juan's Cantina— tamales like your mother cooked."

I imagined Juan's with bright-colored tables, festive music, maybe a stuffed bird above the bar. He sat in a wooden chair with a frothy drink in his hand, gazing at the person across from him, and it wasn't me. I wanted it to be me.

"Did your mother cook tamales?" I asked.

"Excuse me?"

"Never mind."

I wanted to hear him talk. He looked at me out of the side of his eyes. I still held the lighter in my hand. I reread the words.

"Do you go to Juan's often?" I blurted.

"Juan who?"

"Juan. Juan's Cantina."

He looked around, confused.

I clutched the lighter in my hand and wanted so desperately to be with him, to be his date at Juan's.

"Will you buy my tea for me?"

He cocked an eyebrow. A black caterpillar moving up his face.

"I'll give you the money." I jingled the money for the necklace in my hand. "You just hand it to the waiter."

"You're an odd chick."

"Am I?" I had asked, delighted. "Am I an odd chick?"

We sat and drank our tea together without talking and then suddenly he flew backward out of his chair and the watchdog was there snatching my arm and dragging me down the stairs. Shattered glass lay around the table and I could see it had cut the foreigner on his arm, a red slash glistening in the sunlight.

I didn't care. It was the happiest day of my life.

21

Meanwhile Back at the Oasis

THE OASIS WAS DARK AND SILENT WHEN THEY ARRIVED. THERE were no birds chirping, no insects humming and the lunatic did not emerge to take their camels.

Where is he? Ouma frowned. He is always here.

The moment Ouma asked where he was, Lili knew it had been him in the village, him who had kissed her on the roof. The grip, the tickle of the beard, the lips under the hood, the intensity, the pressure—a lunatic named Ben had been the first man to kiss her.

Ouma stood on her tiptoes and looked over the bushes to the lunatic's spot.

The one time we need him and he has decided to leave the oasis.

They unsaddled the camels themselves and used palm leaves to brush off the dirt underneath the saddles. Each took a bucket and walked to the edge of the water. Lili was splashing water on her face and arms when Ouma nudged her.

Look. It's him.

There he was. The lunatic sat across the water, behind several palm trees, hunched over as usual. He had managed to sneak back before her. How was that possible?

Hello, Ouma hollered. The camels are waiting.

He didn't raise his head or acknowledge her voice. He continued to sit, rocking back and forth slightly with the gusts of the wind. Maybe he was hurt or angry with Lili.

Bastard, Ouma said. He is not with this world. And now he is deaf as well.

Midhat?

They turned and Fatima stood in the doorway of her tent, her hands clutching a stack of paper. Her voice was hoarse as if she had been calling for Midhat all day. From the edges of paper that Lili could see, she knew they were the drawings from under the rug, the sketches of penises.

Midhat? she asked again in her rough voice.

He is not here, Ouma said.

Where is he?

He is not back yet.

I must see him.

You cannot see anyone.

Where is Midhat? she screamed and held the pages out in front of her.

Lili cringed. She could unmistakably see what was on the pages.

What is the problem? Ouma asked and walked toward Fatima.

Fatima vanished into her tent. Lili ran up to Ouma and touched her arm.

Come with me, I think the lunatic is hurt.

Ouma gazed back at the inert figure across the oasis.

He looks fine, she said.

Inside the tent, Raja shrieked, but was stopped short. Ouma gave the lunatic one more glance and stepped through the tent flap. Lili followed. In the dim enclosure, Fatima and Raja sat close together on one of the beds. In one hand Fatima held the papers, with the other, she gripped Raja's arm. Raja sat with her head down and did not look up. Fatima clenched Raja's arm tighter and Raja let out a whimper, casting Lili a quick look, a flash of blue in the dark room.

What is the problem? Ouma asked again.

I cannot tell you. You have already lied to me once.

Not me, I have never lied to you, Ouma said. Midhat will not be back for some time. You can tell me.

Do you think I didn't hear you looking at them? She hissed and rattled the papers in Lili's direction. Liar.

Give them to me, Ouma said. I will see what they are.

They are filth. They are against all Mohammed's teachings of not to draw idols.

What sort of idols?

That is what Midhat must see.

He is not here.

Why should I trust you? You will help her.

Help her what?

Do not lie to me.

Give them to me. I cannot see them behind your back.

Fatima slowly brought the papers forward. You will be punished if you lie to me.

Ouma took the papers and opened the curtain to the tent. In the sunlight, Raja's face was streaked and bloated with tears. Ouma peered at the papers and shifted through them slowly, one by one. Her eyes were wide and she stared at each drawing as though it were an incomprehensible object. Raja hung her head so low that Lili could see only the white tip of her nose from under the hood.

Ouma burst out laughing. Raja hung her head even lower.

Why Fatima, Ouma said, they are blank.

Raja looked up, her face drained white, except for the red of her eyes. Fatima stood, spittle forming at the corners of her mouth.

You are lying. I can feel the drawings on the paper. Give them to me.

Ouma shifted the papers and handed Fatima the blank sheets. Fatima ran her fingers over the papers, throwing each one on the floor.

Nothing. There is nothing here. I did not imagine this. You are all cursed. Out of my tent. Now.

Outside, Ouma went straight to the kitchen fire and lit it. She sat on a rock next to it and she and Lili began crumpling the papers and feeding them to the flames. Raja stood behind her, twisting her hands and breathing quickly.

I have something to tell you. I knew. I knew which bowl had the poison in it.

Raja, Ouma said.

And I'm glad she cannot see anymore.

Raja, Lili said.

I had wanted her to die for a long time and finally the perfect time came. She hated me from the day of my wedding. She hates everything about me. She said my eyes were the eyes of Satan. She thought I would give Midhat the child he wants and then I would be the favorite. She thinks it is me who will not take off my veil in front of her, she thinks it is disrespectful, but it is Midhat who forbids me to do so. It is he who makes us hate each other.

You should have poisoned Midhat, said Lili.

Midhat? Then what would happen to us? The two of us, widows together? The thought is too horrible to imagine. Now she has cursed me. She has cursed all of us, we are doomed. All is lost.

Ignorant girl, Ouma fanned the flames. Nothing is lost or doomed.

Raja grabbed the remaining papers and shoved them into the fire all at once. Quick, she said, quick.

Raja, stop, Raja. You've put the fire out.

As Raja put her hands into the fire, frantically shredding the leftover paper into tiny pieces, Lili heard the snort of a camel. Gabriel had arrived.

There, Lili said to Ouma. You see, it was Gabriel behind you.

Ouma whirled around and faced Gabriel, hands on her hips, jaw thrust forward.

Were you spying on me? she demanded.

Why would I spy on you?

Were you following me?

Why would I follow you?

Gabriel eyed Raja. What's wrong with Raja?

Raja stopped shredding.

And where is that lunatic? His gaze swept the lunatic's spot. I need him to take the camel.

He is over there, said Lili. I'll get him for you.

The first gust of the afternoon wind picked up and caught the bits of paper Raja had been shredding, blowing them in tight whirl-winds, little pieces of penises floating round and round. Raja sat frozen, her eyes flicking from left to right as the paper spun in front of her.

Lili thought about the lunatic's lips as she walked toward the other end of the oasis. She wouldn't recognize his robe or beard, but his lips, she could imagine how they would look by the way they felt. Lili walked around the last of the date palms and hesitantly approached his hunched figure.

Hello, she called.

He didn't answer, merely continued to look out over the oasis.

How did you arrive before me?

He still ignored her.

She stepped closer. Was it you? Tell the truth. I'm not mad anymore. I don't want any lies, no more lies.

She stepped closer until she was standing next to him. She smiled at him.

And I'm sorry if I pushed you off the roof. I was surprised. Shocked.

The evening wind began to pick up and he rocked with the gusts. The oasis looked beautiful from this view, sprays of sand lifting off the dunes in lacy sheets. Filmy clouds spread across the azure sky. Lili sat next to him and sighed. They were silent for several moments, watching the ashes from Raja's papers blow up into a funnel above the oasis. He twitched in an odd way that made her think he might really be injured.

Are you all right?

She touched his shoulder. It cracked and he swayed away from her. She squeezed his arm. It rustled in a way that was not flesh. Lili leaped up and he toppled over. The robe was full of weeds. She had been talking to a robe stuffed with straw.

She cursed. Someone touched her from behind and her head flushed with blood. Behind her was the lunatic. His cool brown eyes gazed into hers. Again, she was sure he belonged in the city. His eyes were not far-searching as a desert person's should be, they focused more on the depth of the present. She stared at his mouth. The intensity of his eyes distracted her, she couldn't know for sure. He held his lips in a funny way. He bit his bottom lip, holding it between his teeth so that white marks appeared on the sides.

Was it you?

He chortled and released his lip. It sprung out and looked much too large to be one of the lips that had touched hers. She felt disappointed and reckless.

You know what I've done, don't you?

The brown of his eyes rolled back and his lids closed. His jaw convulsed until he grabbed on to his bottom lip again and held it tightly. He bent over and tugged the straw out of his stuffed robe in handfuls before meticulously folding the garment.

They call you a lunatic.

He leaned over and wrenched his hood over his face in a quick gesture.

Well, are you?

He stood and walked away.

I'm sorry, she said.

On the ground was his folded robe.

You dropped your robe.

He turned and looked back.

You heard me, she said. You heard me.

He snorted and walked to the robe, shaking his head in fast little movements.

Do you have a tongue? she asked him. Can you talk?

When he bent over to pick up the robe, he stayed bent over as if he simply forgot to stand up. She crouched down to look at him. His mouth moved, his eyes implored her. She thought he might be trying to tell her something, she leaned closer and his lips went to hers, that touch, a light flicking of his tongue, drawing energy from her, weakening her legs until she slipped onto her knees.

She stayed on the ground for quite some time after he left. The sand felt cool. Gusts of wind lifted the grains, tattooed her calves and coated her tongue. She thought maybe she could not speak anymore.

22

Always Look Your Best

"Always look your best," was Madame Mer's motto. So, every morning we bathed, twisted, curled and primped our hair, then dressed in our finest.

Madame Mer taught us to be what she thought men wanted. She was always right. The walk, the talk, the look—she had it down to a formula.

There was an unwritten list of beauty tricks she taught us. Not too much eye contact, until the right moment, and then, *bam*, let them have it—intense eye contact that made men heave with desire. A smoothing of hair that brought the arm up to its best vantage and in the moment of smoothing, a slight twist of graceful neck and a glimpse of profile. A stroll that never hurried and commanded attention with its rolling of hips and pressing of buttocks.

In the morning, before we bathed, we marched around the stone floor for twenty minutes in our robes with a ten-dirham coin between our buttocks. Twenty minutes with ten dirhams will give the stride of a princess, Madame Mer used to say. Shoulders back, elbows turned slightly out, stomach stretched flat. She would follow us with her polished cane, and if the coin fell, rattling to the floor, she would rap the back of our heels sharply. Right on the Achilles tendon. Before the bathing, we were followed up the stairs, Madame Mer close behind.

Walking up stairs with a ten-dirham coin between your buttocks is no easy feat.

When we were sent home with our husbands, we were sent with instructions. Never let him see you in an unflattering pose. In particular, in stages of undress. Shoes always come off first, if there is any walking (parading) to do, they must be put back on, but only if they are high heels. Shirt comes off before skirt, and bra before panties. For those girls unfortunate enough to have freckles, a solution of bleach and water was to be put on the skin for twenty minutes a day. For bags under the eyes: hemorrhoid cream. It tightens the blood vessels. For those with weak nails, a glass of gelatin. When reading a book, tape across the eyebrows to stop the frown. Mayonnaise once a week for shiny hair . . .

Madame Mer told us we did not have the brains or breeding to make it in the world, so we would have to rely on our looks. I am blessed with a face and a body that please men, so why shouldn't I have used them? In the desert, they are worthless. If only she could see me now.

23

The Plan

Midhat sat outside in the early morning coolness, banging on the metal kettle with a rock until everyone emerged from the tents and stood in front of him.

People have been stealing my camels, he said, twitching his chin.

They looked at the camels.

How many are missing? asked Gabriel.

None are missing, they have been returned. This must stop. They are my camels. Midhat looked at their blank faces and threw the kettle to the ground in a fury. Imbeciles. We do not steal each other's property at the oasis.

He stared at the kettle until his breathing settled down. The grand plan has become clear to me, he said calmly.

Plan?

Have you forgotten so quickly? Fools. It is the will of Allah. The plan to steal from the Russians. I now understand what is required of us.

Us? Lili's eyes darted to Ouma's.

Each of you will perform according to his or her talent.

This is not theater.

I will reveal your roles . . . later. Yes, all of you, including . . . you. He looked at Lili.

I have no talents, Lili said.

You must be able to do something.

It didn't matter one way or the other, because she would escape this poky little oasis with the Russians, long before that. But what talent did she have? Converse with men of all ages and nationalities, tower above all of humankind and . . . sing. Madame Mer had taught her to sing. I can sing, she said.

Fine.

You want me to sing to the Russians?

What can you sing?

Beatles?

No, something they will be drawn to.

A lullaby.

Good. The Russians will arrive in three days' time and the grand plan will be put into action. Remember, it is our desert we are fighting for. Right, Raja?

Raja fingered the green feathered charm around her neck and stared at the ground. I will help my people, she said.

Good girl, Raja. I knew you'd understand. When the Russians come back, we rob them. Pirates of the Sahara. Rumors of us will spread throughout Morocco. Yes, pirates of the Sahara and we will be feared by all.

Midhat, Ouma said, planting her feet squarely and crossing her arms. Are you an arms dealer?

Of course not.

Then what is this deal with the Russians?

Who says I'm making a deal?

We have heard.

It's part of my plan. I am a trader, I trade things.

You trade arms?

Of course not.

What have you promised the Russians to get them to the oasis?

A trade.

Arms.

Midhat pursed his bowed lips. Not arms.

His lips were the sort of lips that started fights, that made men want to flatten them, to still their movements and silence their words. Lili wanted to punch them right in the center.

Legs? Ouma suggested.

Lili smiled. She looked around for the lunatic. He sat in the bushes facing the water, but she couldn't tell if it was him or a robe full of straw. Midhat brought his arms out in front of his stomach and contemplated them. He was slick, like a used-car salesman.

Not arms, he insisted. Money for land mines. Land mines, not guns.

Do you really see a difference? The government uses over a million land mines to keep the desert people out of the desert, and now you want to sell land mines to the Russians so they can kill the remaining desert people still inside the desert?

We are stealing them back.

No and no.

After you play your role in the plan, Midhat said, ignoring Ouma and fixing each of them with his beady eyes, your dreams will become reality.

Gabriel snorted. Tell us, Midhat, what are our dreams?

You dream the same dream. You all dream of a new life. Money to cross the Strait of Gibraltar. Spain: bullfights, flamenco dancers, rioja, paella—

You are not truly of the desert, Ouma shook herself. You are not even of Morocco. You are only of yourself.

I have made sacrifices for you. He thrust his foot forward. Money is a passport away from the oasis.

Lili put her hand to her chest and clasped the bag with the Arab's chains. Her ticket out, she didn't need Midhat's money. She would agree to participate in his plan and then leave with the Russians.

Ouma wagged her index finger from side to side. I will never help you.

I saved your life, Midhat said quietly.

You are collecting lives. I will not be collected.

Lili walked toward the water and sat with her toes almost touching the edge of the pool. Inside the bag were the chains, still glittering and heavy. The wind began to blow and she could only hear vague snatches of the argument.

Raja sat down next to her and raised her face to the sky, smiling underneath her veil. The green feathers moved with the wind as if they were alive.

Raja, what happened to the bird?

She searched the sky. Bird?

The green bird that fell from the sky onto your head the day I arrived.

Raja touched the top of her head. It died.

Died?

It was almost dead when it fell. Almost. I needed the feathers for a talisman. Raja touched the feathers with her fingertip reverently. They are good luck, you are good luck. I thought your fate was to be the same as the green bird.

The feathers were a fresh green that did not exist in the desert. The green made the blue of Raja's eyes so intense, Lili had to lean away. Lili stared at Raja's hands. They were small with square palms and round fingers of varying lengths. The nails were rough from work. Could it have been Raja who saved her?

If you saved the green bird, did you save me?

I did not save the green bird. That's why I didn't mind when Midhat told me you were not to be in this world any longer. Do you see?

But, the green bird fell out of the sky and died from heatstroke.

It did not die because of the heat, it died because I wanted it to.

You killed the green bird? You killed it?

For the feathers. Fatima gave me the evil eye to stop me from getting pregnant. I needed to break it and put a curse of my own on her.

And then you tried to kill me?

It was not my choice.

I am not a green bird. No more deaths, only for those who welcome them.

You are not the green bird, you are alive. And I thank you and the green bird, for you have brought me luck. I am pregnant.

The palm trees whispered above. Raja tilted her head and looked up to thank the heavens. Lili understood the blue color of Raja's eyes—the color of madness. Perhaps the insane can see what the sane cannot.

Lili looked across the water. The lunatic sat as he had so many times before. There was nothing to ground her in reality in the desert. Was it possible she was dead already and didn't know it? She had heard death was like life, complete with dreams. She willed the lunatic to look up, twist his neck, scratch his head, to even breathe deeply so she would know he was really there.

24

Worries

Suddenly I have become a worrier. I, who have never worried, merely floated along in the stream of life. Existed on the peripheral. The thing I worry most about is the real me. What happens if the real me emerges and I don't like myself?

Maybe I'm nasty and bitter or an absolute harlot. Maybe I kick dogs or trample new flowers.

Every day, I discover more ways I am not myself. What I know so far is that I am not a vegetarian, my hair is not meant to be blond, I am not a Muslim. There are two people in me trying to be the only one, with my body stuck in the middle.

I can't stay here in Morocco, not with the Arab dead, or alive. Where will I go? London treated me like a slow-blooded hound, sniffing at me then backing away. Paris had Notre Dame, which brought on nightmares rampant with skeletal flying buttresses and hideous gargoyles. New York was too fast, everything a blur of yellow, black and gray—except the Statue of Liberty, an enormous surreal doll floating in the water. In Barcelona there were vestiges of Gaudi, or gaudy, as the Arab called him and hallucinations of melting angels. Lisbon is too close to Morocco, I want to be far away. Amsterdam with its labyrinth of canals, haze of smoke and careening bikes would only confuse me.

And Russia? Babushkas dressed in black, hair covered with frayed handkerchiefs, wooden carts commandeered by vodka-driven men, stacks of rubles worth one loaf of bread—if you could find it. The Russians, bitter with life and stalled expectations. My mother and I had a big rat living in our flat with us. We would crumple newspapers around the floor so we could hear it crawl into the room and then we would leap out of bed, shouting and screaming. I can't go back to the rat.

Perhaps I am more of a gypsy than I ever knew. Maybe there will be no home, except for where I am at that moment. Like the no-mads, when there is no more, I will leave.

25

Ouma Kidnapping

THEY CAME AT DAWN, HALF A DOZEN OF THEM WITH DARK ROBES and whispers that disappeared with the wind. Camels sighed and footsteps sank into the night. They knew exactly where Ouma slept, they had been watching. Lili heard a slight rustling, a muffled protest, and by the time she looked, Ouma was gone.

Lili ran out of the tent.

Ouma?

There was no reply, only many footprints in the sand. Night hung in the air by a thread, luminous stars still sharp in the deep blue sky. Lili turned slowly in a circle, calling to Ouma again and again until her legs shook and she dropped onto her knees in the cold sand.

Lili?

She opened her eyes and saw Gabriel crouched in front of her.

They've taken Ouma, she said.

Who?

I don't know.

She must be here.

He stood without moving for a moment. He cupped his ears and listened briefly. Then he crouched before Lily again.

Why would someone take Ouma?

It is not our business, Midhat said. His outline stood over them with his hands on his hips.

Gabriel straightened his legs, stood as tall as his frame would allow and faced Midhat. Where is Ouma? he asked.

Midhat swept his hand across the glowing horizon.

You knew, Lili said. Why didn't you stop them?

Why should I stop them?

They forced her to go.

No matter, she is gone.

Please.

It is not for us to be involved.

She is Ouma.

She has dishonored her family.

Her husband will kill her. We need to go after her, steal her back. She is one of us.

One of us? What does that mean? What are we?

Hsuma, shame on you, Midhat.

It is not possible.

It will be practice for us. For the Russians.

She's not my wife.

We must get her back, or I won't participate in your plan.

Midhat tilted his head and exhaled loudly. Practice for the Russians?

Yes.

Then we will go to her village.

Once more Lili found herself trotting across the desert on a camel. Back through the red river beds, ink-colored stones, steely thorns, back to the one-eyed camel man, back to the kiss.

Midhat led them into the village and down a dark pathway. The streets had been washed of their blood. He stopped behind a house with white laundry strung across the alley and jabbed his finger at the house. Two bright-colored shirts, both child-sized, dangled in the middle of all the white. The windows were dark.

Midhat put a finger to his lips and motioned for them to follow him. They crept down a dirt path and peered over a rock fence. In front of them was a courtyard full of gossiping women and romping children. On the front door of the house hung a bronze knocker, in the shape of the hand of Fatima, to ward off the evil eye. The windows were open and pale curtains drifted in the sunlight. Lili wondered if Ouma had made the curtains and if she had been happy living there.

A small boy ran in tight circles until he staggered and fell onto the ground, laughing. An old woman picked him up and carried him into the house. Midhat ducked and pulled everyone down behind him. He crept to one of the windows and peered in. A piece of cut crystal hung from inside and caught the light, sending shards of color along the dull walls.

Lili looked at Midhat's crouching form and felt there was something deceitful in it. She was sure Ouma was not to be found here, in this house. Quietly, she tread down the path and retraced her footsteps through the village.

Her feet seemed to know where they were going and she was more alarmed than surprised when she reached the house where she had seen Midhat and the Russians. The shutters were closed tight. In the desert, Ouma had told her she was more afraid of the Russians than her husband. And the whispers in the night. Her husband wouldn't have been so scheming.

Lili cautiously stuck her head up over the windowsill and squinted through the wooden slats. Nothing. The room was dark. A door opened toward the back of the room and light shone through it. Lili blinked and there she saw Ouma in the far corner, seated on the floor, hands tied behind her. Hair hung in front of her face and a line of dried blood bisected her lips. A ginger chicken pecked at her feet. Lily felt a pain dart through her chest.

Between Ouma and Lili, stood a silver-haired man with his back to Lili. He paced back and forth, tapping a thick stick against his thigh. The door slammed shut.

This is not Ouma's family, Lili whispered to herself. Oh, Allah ister.

A hand clasped her shoulder from behind and another covered her mouth. Her head was tilted gently back.

Gabriel.

He released her.

Where is Midhat? she asked.

Still back at the house.

Does he know you're gone?

He must now.

Guess who's here.

He stretched his little neck up to the window and brought it back down in a flash.

The Russians.

And?

Ouma?

Yes.

How did you know?

I didn't. I just didn't trust Midhat.

Fools, fools. A harsh whisper came from behind them. Why are you here? Why did you leave me to save Ouma by myself?

Lili turned and shot Midhat a ferocious glare. Ouma is here.

Impossible. She's back at the other house. Hurry.

Look for yourself.

Midhat crept to the window and inched his head up. It snapped back down.

It is the Russians.

I have seen Ouma.

Oh Allah, why have you burdened me with such jesters? All my plans are ruined. We cannot interfere.

I will rescue her, Lili said.

You cannot. This was to be practice before the Russians, now it is simply the Russians. If we are caught, everything is gone.

Stop whining, Midhat, and do something.

Do? What can I do? Me with my missing toes.

You create a distraction. Get the guards away from here.

What am I to do? Shriek? Cry? Laugh?

Do you want help with your plan, or not?

My plan. My plan is shattered. Ruined. Allah preserve me, he said, drawing his hood over his head and disappearing down the alley.

Lili and Gabriel squatted in the street and waited for Midhat's diversion. Lili was aware of Gabriel near her. He smelled fresh despite the heat, sort of a soapy, airy smell and she wondered how that was possible after riding on a camel through the desert. She looked at him sideways and lowered her gaze to his hands. Those hands with smooth fingernails. He must have fallen for her when he found her in the desert.

He caught her looking at him. I told you Ouma was trouble, he said.

It's not her fault they kidnapped her.

Actually, it is.

How can you say that? She—

Listen, Lili, I need something from you.

Not now, Gabriel, later.

Yes, later. Do something for me.

She looked at him suspiciously. What?

Arrange for Raja to meet me. By herself.

Why?

You know why.

Lili shook her head.

She is the one.

The one?

The one I . . .

Raja is the one you love?

A serene smile crept across his face. Lili felt wounded. Not that she wanted him, but why didn't he love her? She was too tall. She slouched closer to the ground and fixed her gaze on Gabriel.

Stay away from Raja. She is pregnant with Midhat's child.

Gabriel flushed. Drops of sweat appeared in a row. Pregnant? Dios mio.

This is what she prayed for. This is what Midhat wanted. Go back to Spain and find a wife. This is not for you.

It is more for me than you think.

What are you saying?

She loves me.

She has a husband. Love doesn't matter.

The sweat trickled down the side of his face. His tongue snaked out and caught one of the drops. It is mine, he said.

No.

Yes.

It will be obvious, Midhat will know—

An enormous bang shook the ground, tiles slid off roofs and pigeons flapped in the air. Shouts rang out from the house. Three men ran out the door and down the alley, guns drawn. Lili and Gabriel waited for a moment and then walked nonchalantly to the front door.

Someone grabbed Lili from behind and pressed on her throat until black specks began to gather around the edges of her vision. She focused on a lizard clinging to the ceiling, a translucent body with great black eyes that seemed ready to impart a piece of wisdom to Lili, something she needed to know desperately, but just as she could have grasped its message, at the very moment of delivery, it was gone and the blackness took over.

Lili opened her eyes and Gabriel stood over her. She searched the ceiling for the lizard. There was nothing. Next to her lay a guard, his hands tied neatly behind him, knees bent and ankles connected to his hands in a sort of taut bow position. And a gag in his mouth.

Gabriel, said Lili. Did you do that?

Never mind. You get yourself in some bad situations.

Look at him.

Lili walked unsteadily to the door in the back of the room. She flung it open and there was Ouma. Both of her eyes were swollen shut. They opened a crack and glistened.

Lili, she said. Moisture oozed along the cracks of her lids. You found me.

Ouma.

Drops of water splashed on Lili's hand and she was surprised to find tears falling from her eyes. The ginger chicken ran in circles, flying against the walls in puffs of feathers and squawking.

Quick, Gabriel said. That damn chicken.

Lili tried to help Ouma up, but found Ouma was bound to a stake in the ground. She fiddled with the ropes, they were in tight knots.

We need a knife, she said.

Lili turned around and saw Midhat with an enormous knife raised above him. She screamed, and with a great whoosh, Midhat brought the knife down and sliced off the chicken's head. Blood spurted everywhere. The chicken's body twitched and jerked its way around the room. Midhat ran to Lili and covered her mouth.

She must be dead, Midhat said to Gabriel. It is the only way. Do you understand?

Lili sunk her teeth into his hand. He yelped and threw her against the wall. Ouma kicked at him with her foot.

They must think she's dead, he said and lunged for Lili, who screamed again.

Lili, quiet. Shut up. He's right, Gabriel said. Listen to him. Pull out some of Ouma's hair.

Midhat grabbed Ouma's long hair at the scalp and whacked it off. Ouma quietly sobbed to herself.

They must think she is dead, Gabriel said. They will think her family has come to claim her and to kill her. It is the only way.

Lili thought for a moment. Damn, he was right. If they thought she was dead, both the Russians and her family would leave her alone.

I understand.

The room turned into a frenzy of blood smearing, hair scattering and clothing ripping. Gabriel opened a knife and cut the ropes away from Ouma. Lili and Gabriel each took an arm and dragged her out of the room.

26

Misogynist

It took me four years to see what the Arab was — a misogynist. A woman hater. And it wasn't even my own discovery, a woman at the disco told me.

She had leaned over the table and shouted, "He is very good looking."

I looked at the Arab and tried to see what she saw. He leaned against the bar, arms crossed, one hip slouched lower than the other. In the dark bar, his skin seemed even darker. His eyebrows met together in an angry V. He watched two girls dancing in front of him. They were aware of him watching and put a little extra effort into their movements.

"But," she continued, "he is a woman hater."

Suddenly, I saw how it was. She was right. He hated women.

His face was the kind of face a woman is attracted to, strong masculine with a hint of cruelty. When he looked at women they responded and they were rewarded with a sneering sort of disgust. He kept his distance, yet could not stay away. He never flirted, he commanded. And once a woman showed a fondness for him, he was gone. He has never been with another woman that I know of, except his wives. I know he didn't like me, I simply held his interest longer than the rest of the wives.

Possibly his interest was held by the crazy things he dreamt up for me to do. Several months ago, we passed a beggar woman and he asked me how I would like to become someone like her. I told him I didn't know, maybe it wasn't so bad.

He grabbed my wrist and forced me to the ground several meters away from the beggar woman and laid out one of his handkerchiefs, the ones with his initials and braided corners, and set it in front of me.

"This is what you will be doing when I tire of you," he said.

He backed away and sat on a bench some distance from me. The beggar woman hissed in my direction and scuttled off, farther away. Still he made me stay, crouched in my position, the handkerchief spread in front of me like dirty underwear.

When the first coin hit the cloth, I felt amazed. Exhilarated. The first money I had ever earned. I picked it up and held it in the palm of my hand, weighing it, and then another coin fell. Every time someone walked by, I stared at the person, willing him or her to drop a little something on the handkerchief.

The Arab got tired of waiting around and walked over to collect me. "You're a natural," he said. "How did it feel?"

I didn't answer and he peered at my face. His eyes narrowed when he saw the excitement shining in them. The money was held tight in my fist. It was worth nothing, not even a tenth of the price of a drink at the disco. It didn't matter. I wanted it—I had earned it. The Arab was good at knowing what I was thinking and he took my fist and forced out the coins. He threw them into the gutter.

"That was nothing," he said. "Wouldn't even buy you a gin and tonic."

He was always furious when I didn't seem to learn from his lessons. I did learn though.

27

The Arab and the Lover

OUMA HAD BEEN ASLEEP FOR ALMOST TWENTY-FOUR HOURS WHEN
the wind began to blow in earnest. Dust churned high into the afternoon sky, saturating the air so the oasis appeared to be encased in a
big dun-colored bubble. Heat pressed aggressively against Lili's skin.

The Russians would arrive at the oasis tomorrow and Lili needed to
prepare her plea for escape. She sat in the doorway of the tent and tried
to piece together a Russian phrase. She tried to think of her name, her
real Russian name, the one her mother had given her. Vlada? Anna?
Irena? She had lost her Russian name when she toppled into the Bosphorus. It lay hidden in the oily depths, among metal cans, discarded
sabers and seaweed twisting in the ebb and flow.

She licked her lips and tasted the fine layer of dust that covered
them. Out of the corner of her eye, she saw Ouma's eyes open.

As soon as Lili turned to look, they closed.

Ouma?

Ouma continued to lie there with her eyes closed, breathing steadily.

Ouma, everyone thinks you are dead and you are safe now.

Lili stared hard at Ouma's eyelids. Maybe she had imagined her
eyes were open.

I saw your son.

Ouma's eyes opened wide and she scowled. What does it matter?

137

You're not happy to be rescued.

Her face twitched and her eyes flooded. Where?

In the village. At your old house.

Ouma sat up cautiously and Lili saw the bruises that had appeared on her skin overnight. The pupils of her eyes were tiny in their swollen pockets. Lili moved to help her.

No, I am only a little sore. How do you know it was my house?

Midhat took us. There was a little boy.

My son. What did he do?

He ran in . . .

Yes. She closed her eyes for a moment. He loves to run in circles.

And he laughed.

I know, he lives without me. Fat tears slid out of Ouma's inflamed eyes. He is a boy. I am not worried he will be treated badly.

That is your husband's family. What about your family?

My family is in the refugee camps on the other side of the wall. In Algeria. We've been split for twenty-five years. My mother doesn't know where my father is. They told us, the desert people, we could vote on whether to be part of Morocco or not. They lied, so we wait. Year after year.

She spat at the wall, but no moisture came out of her mouth.

Why would Midhat take you to my husband's family?

He was looking for you.

He knew where I was.

Yes, I think so.

Wind rocked the tent almost tenderly. Lili rubbed her fingers along her cheekbones to feel the haze of dust fixed to her damp skin.

The wind has arrived.

Wind is good for the Sahara, everything will be new.

It's so dry, how long will it last?

There is no answer, Ouma said.

She lay back on her bed and stared at the ceiling. If my lover had been here, they never would have dared to kidnap me. Something has happened to him. I am afraid.

Why would the Russians want you?

They don't want me, they want what I know.

What do you know?

I know where the rebels are who are blowing up their investments.

Oh.

Something has happened to him. Something bad.

The Russians arrive tomorrow, Lili said.

And I will help Midhat with his plan.

What?

I owe him.

That's crazy. Do you realize it is the same Russians he is talking about stealing from?

They are the only Russians.

It is too dangerous. What if they discover you are alive?

I'll wear a veil. They are stupid, they think everyone in a robe looks the same. My lover would have never worked with the Russians. He hated them. He thought they were taking over the country, stealing all the resources.

Did he hate all Russians?

Yes, all Russians. Have you ever seen a good Russian?

Lili wanted to say, me, what about me? Am I a good Russian? Am I a Russian?

The wind increased its intensity. Lili went to the door and stepped outside, shutting the door behind her. The sun was trying to prick the dun-colored bubble, but the sand had reduced the sun to an inept ball of fire, far away, its flames dulled. Lili smiled at its inability to claim the sky. At this rate, if the Russians did arrive, she wouldn't be able to see them.

She couldn't see the lunatic, whether he sat curled in a ball or was inside the shelter with the camels. The stinging sand forced her back in the tent.

What about your husband, Lili? You are the kind of girl someone marries.

Lili laughed.

Why aren't you married?

I am. I was.

Where is he now?

He is gone.

He will be back to find you. They always come back.

I don't know if he will be back. Lili felt guilty. No lies, she told herself.

I lied, she said. He called me his wife, but I wasn't, not really. And I'm glad. He's not someone I would choose to marry.

I would like to marry my lover. I had no choice with my husband. It's terrible to want someone so much, but it's worse without it. Ouma looked at Lili with her bruised eyes. My lover is the reason I live.

Lili thought about the Arab. He was not why she lived, but he was why she wanted to die. In fact she couldn't remember anything good about the Arab. Or even anything horrible. Hopefully, he would disappear from her memory entirely.

You must think I am a bad mother.

I don't know anything about mothers.

Maybe I am.

From what I know, you seem more good than bad.

Yeah?

Ouma, do you know why I am here?

You are Aisha Qandisha.

Lili thought for a moment. Was she Aisha Qandisha? Jenni of the Oasis? Do you really want to know why I am here?

No.

The door flew open and Midhat crashed into the tent. Lili recoiled and pressed herself against the wall. Midhat frightened her. He had become crazier and crazier. She expected him to foam at the mouth or lunge at them with his knife.

Are you ready for the Russians? He stared belligerently at Ouma.

I am ready. Ouma refused to meet his eyes. Thank you.

It was nothing, not too much of an explosion.

What? Ouma said. Thank you for saving me. What explosion?

Midhat created the diversion, so the guards left you and we could save you, Lili said.

You mean you set off a bomb in the middle of my village?

Well, uh, yes.

How could you?

I . . . I didn't do it. I didn't have time to make a diversion.

If you didn't do it, who did it?

Well, it wasn't the Russians, they wouldn't have diverted themselves from the house.

Midhat started twitching his chin. I was stacking a pile of camel chips to burn. I figured a fire would be fine distraction, when all of a sudden, *bang*, there was a huge explosion several blocks away. Not my bang, not my bang at all.

He turned and went out the door.

I don't trust that man, said Ouma.

That night, the storm blew soft piles of sand through every crack and crevice in the tent. Lili lay on her back, hot wind moving over her body in soft tremors. The currents awakened a force in her, a ferocity that made her sweat in rivers down the sides of her body.

Ouma lay sleeping, peacefully unaware. Gusts pulsed against the walls, inflating and deflating them in giant breaths. Lili's fists clenched the blanket until she was sure blood would pour forth. She burst out of her bed and ran outside. Sand blew in sharp needle pricks against her skin. She wrapped herself in the blanket and headed around the oasis, toward the lunatic.

The violence in her matched that of the storm outside and she screamed out loud in a pure frenzy. She didn't see him with the camels, where else would he be? She headed toward the palm trees and when she stepped on what she thought was ground, there was nothing and her foot went down, down into a wetness that made her twist and fall. She and her blanket had dropped straight into the pond. A film of sand covered the water so it looked identical to the land. Here she was, the duckling following after the man of her first kiss. Her mouth opened and she laughed and laughed and her laugh turned into a scream that was carried away with the wind.

She felt him rather than saw him and when she looked up, he stood watching her. As much as her scream may have dissipated into the storm, he certainly heard it from where he stood. His hood flapped around his head, covering most of his face except for his mouth, which was covered by one hand. She thought she heard a laugh. Was the lunatic laughing at her? If he couldn't speak, could he laugh?

She stood and tried to gracefully wrap the blanket around her. It wouldn't cooperate. It hung down like a lead weight and dragged out of her hands toward the water. The lunatic flung off his robe in one motion and offered it to her while turning his head away. She dropped the blanket in the water, the sand biting at her wet skin until his robe covered her.

He hunched into himself and walked away. She watched him lumber into the scrub and then saw why she had not noticed him before. He disappeared into a very small dome-shaped tent underneath the bushes. Lili's hair whipped about her head.

The moon's obscure shape shone through the hazy air.

She ran through the sand to his tent, stopping outside with a skid. He opened the flap and peered out at her. She stooped over and wriggled inside. He tied the flap down, without looking at her, while the wind howled above them. A tiny candle inside a jar dangled from the ceiling, suspended with raw twine.

He slowly removed the robe and touched his tongue to the bone between her breasts and licked a straight line to her neck, curving around her throat until he reached her lips. She tasted the fine sand from her body. A frantic growl drove its way from her throat and she bit his bottom lip, holding it until he became still and his breathing became ragged and uncontrollable.

Only afterward did he look her in the eyes. As if the physical contact had been too painful for him to face. Lili found she couldn't meet his gaze. His eyes were dark and too deep and she worried she would drown in them. She dropped her eyes and nervously tugged at his chest hair.

The blanket was still wet and heavy when she wrapped it around her body again. Outside, the fierce wind flung granules of sand against her face.

28

The High Atlas

AFTER THE PREDICTION OF THE SHUWAFA AND THE ARAB'S DECISION to take me to the desert, we drove across the Atlas Mountains. It was unusual that the watchdog was not with us. I noticed a vulnerability in the Arab, a vulnerability that I hadn't seen before, and it irritated him that I noticed.

We drove through twenty shades of bleakness. First, there was the regular scrub desert pierced by stunted acacia trees. On the Marrakech side, we were dwarfed by mammoth blue-black slabs of rock. The people disappeared. Rock turned to barren megaliths, the soil lightened into smoother terrain covered with chunks of rock. After the peaks, we wove down through drop-dead cliffs, a few fertile valleys and back to the desert. We drove for hours into the flat desolation.

This is where the argument started. "This is hell," I said.

The Arab frowned and clenched the steering wheel. "You're not seeing it through the right eyes," he said.

I tried to see it through his eyes. I rolled down the window and stared at the desiccated riverbeds, the clusters of stones, the tornadoes of dust whirling into the air.

He continued, "The desert has a lot to offer."

I snorted, "Dust and rocks."

He narrowed his eyes. "Minerals and beauty."

I couldn't argue about the minerals. Everyone knew about the fight between the government and the desert people. Both wanted control of this wind-blasted inferno and one wanted independence.

The Arab said to take another look. "There is beauty to be seen."

I gazed out the window. "This is hell," I repeated.

"I am never surprised by your stupidity. You know nothing of hell, because you live in heaven. Everyone's hell will be created on judgment day and if this is hell for you, this is where you'll be."

He stopped the car. "This is heaven to me. Now, get out of the car and wait for me here. I have business."

Of course I refused. I thought he was going to leave me in hell. It turned out he did.

29

It's Time

THE SUN WAS BACK WITH A VENGEANCE, A BULLY OF A SUN, PUNISHING everything with cruel sharp rays. The rage of the night hovered far, far away. With the wind banished, the landscape was smoothed over, downy as velvet, scorched to blackness, so quiet, silence was a sound. Debris lay against the tents and mounds of sand buried everything that was anything.

Lili felt as if the storm had ruthlessly charged through her body and left something less than before. Burned her outer layer and left her floating, numb, a derelict shell.

She would betray the oasis and thwart Midhat's plan. She would break her promise to Ouma, her word that she would have nothing to do with the Russians. She had to do this. The Russians had to be warned, they were her people and her only scheme for escaping this desert hell.

Raja broke the stillness, racing toward her, robe fluttering, eyes sparking. I have had a vision, she said breathlessly. I have seen the face of my son.

Son? You don't have a son.

I found this in the desert, a talisman. There are magical things buried beneath all this sand. She held out a flat, bread-loaf-sized object. And I saw his face in it.

Lili took it from Raja and inspected it. It was plastic and gray and looked like a dismembered flipper. Recessed into one side was a weather-beaten mirror scratched by sand and dulled by heat.

Raja continued, I was blinded momentarily. And then his face appeared. Allah has forgiven me for Fatima's eyes and bestowed a blessing on my son.

She held the mirror in front of Lili's eyes. The sky shifted in the reflection and Lili too was blinded until she adjusted the angle of the mirror. A face appeared, her face—at least she thought it was her face, for it was completely distorted. Her cheeks bulged out and her forehead appeared swollen.

Raja clutched the charm to her chest. Midhat has said my son will be a visionary.

Why would you believe him?

He knows. Only a man with great baraka can survive a viper and a land mine.

Raja, Raja, what do you think Midhat will say when he sees the baby?

He will be happy and he won't want to kill me anymore.

No. I don't think so. I don't think he will be happy to have a baby that looks like Gabriel with pale skin and light hair.

Raja held her charm to the sky. I can see my son again, she said.

It was like the mirror Lili had seen once in Madrid at a circus. Along with the geek who ate live chickens and the man who swallowed sticks of fire, it was the most memorable part. The House of Mirrors. She had loved it, the way it made her look fat and then thin and then, remarkably short. So short she was practically a dwarf, and she had liked it. For nearly an hour she had sat before the mirror, until the Arab had had to come back into the House of Mirrors, repay the entrance fee, and then forcibly pull her outside.

And what do you see? That your son looks like you?

The baby will look like Midhat, the father.

But the father will be Gabriel, not Midhat.

Midhat is my husband, so Midhat will be the father. Husband and father, they are the same.

Oh, Raja. Do you really believe that?

Raja's jaw began to tremble.

Believe me, Raja, it is not as you think.

Midhat is the father, but there were many who helped me.

Many who . . . My god, Raja. The drawings?

Yes, most of them.

You could be in a lot of trouble.

The drawings were wrong and they were destroyed and then my prayers were answered.

I'm not talking about the drawings, I'm talking about the men.

You told me to.

What?

Yes, you told me to use different men.

I didn't. Lili thought back to the conversation. I told you to try a different means.

Yes, different mens.

No, no, no. I didn't—

You did.

—say that. Not mens: means. A different way to get pregnant, maybe a different position or time of the month or—

Allah ister, what are you telling me?

Raja, listen. There is a good chance that the baby will not look like Midhat and he will know it was from another man.

No . . .

Gabriel wants to speak to you alone.

Why? What have I done to him?

It's not that, he says he loves you.

No, she shook her head rapidly back and forth. He is obsessed. Never.

Why not?

I cannot. What if Midhat found out?

You've done more than talk to him alone.

I never spoke and I kept my veil on. I never looked at him.

Lili thought of the lunatic and how he hadn't looked at her. Was that his way of denying that anything happened? Eye contact could say more than sex ever could. Next time she would make sure he stared into her eyes.

Lili pried the charm from Raja's hands and held it up to the sky to look at herself again. Light shattered in the mirror like a desert-born aurora borealis. She saw the Lili of three weeks ago, Lili of the Arab, Lili of Casablanca. The charm dropped from her hands. Raja gave a little cry and picked it up. Lili knew exactly what the charm really was because she had reapplied her lipstick enough times in it. It was the visor from the Arab's car.

Every molecule of moisture had been sucked out of the sky, the desert floor wasted by carnivorous winds and the sun rose higher, spreading its poison with a new thickness. Lili rubbed her fingers together, two dry corn husks chaffing against each other. The sun absorbed the earth, drawing it up with its tentacles.

I will spontaneously combust, Lili said out loud to no one.

The lunatic dug out the camel stalls, tossing each shovel of sand slowly over his shoulder, his hunched form the only movement on the still horizon. Lili couldn't reconcile this stooped man with the one in the domed tent. It had been pure madness to run after such a person. Or maybe it was that he couldn't speak, could never reveal the details with a sardonic laugh or twitch of the lip. But even as she thought these thoughts, her body went back to the tent, she felt her teeth biting his lip, tearing at his beard and she wanted more, much more.

It was under searing, pristine afternoon skies that the Russians arrived. Three of them. Lili could see them approaching the oasis, small puffs of dust rising and settling around them.

Stupid Russians, again mules in the desert, Midhat said.

He turned and saw Ouma standing there watching them arrive. Dread washed over his face and with a quick movement, he tackled

Ouma and shoved her into her tent, where they both fell onto the floor next to Lili.

Midhat stood up, dusted himself and took Ouma's elbow to help her up, but she jabbed him quickly in the stomach and a blast of air escaped from his mouth.

Please, he said smiling and obsequious, where is your robe? They are here. They are here.

Leave me alone.

I may have overreacted slightly. Now please. And we must be nice to them. Generous.

How nice? asked Ouma.

Obviously, it is best if you stay in your tent.

You are a traitor, dealing with the Russians, she mumbled and glared at Midhat.

Not now, the robe. Or you place all of us in danger. Remember all that I have done for you. He looked desperately around the room and asked Lili, where is her robe?

Lili looked around the tent, but found no robe.

Ouma sat up and held her head in her hands and cried, My lover, my lover, l-qamra . . . What did you do with him?

Him who? He peered out of the tent. Quick, quick, he urged and ran outside, saying, Welcome comrades, welcome to our oasis. Ahlan wa sahlan.

Ouma slapped the palm of her hand against her fist. Bastard, calling Russians our friends. I used to consider Midhat an annoying man. Now I think he is a dangerous hypocrite, he and his toes.

Ouma, for me, put on your robe, pleaded Lili. Look, I'm wearing mine.

These are the same men who kidnapped me. I will not come out of the tent. They are stealing the minerals from our desert. Our desert. Ouma's voice shook. I want to kill them.

Lili tied a veil around her face and walked outside. Midhat stood grinning at the Russians, wringing his hands. They drooped in front of him, shoulders rounded, skin parched, staring at him bleakly.

Tea, he clapped his hands in the direction of Raja's tent. Tea for our fine visitors. Please, there is a place for you to wash over there.

The bald man spoke. He had a turban clumsily wrapped around his head. So hot, he said.

It is the desert.

It is the devil's inferno.

She will take you. Midhat offered Lili's services with an open palm.

Lili shrank into her robe and smiled. This would be the perfect opportunity to talk to the Russians. She motioned for the Russians to follow her. They trudged behind, mules following, footsteps sinking deep into the scalding sand.

A few clippings of mint lay floating in the lucent water of the rock basin and the bald man looked as though he might cry. They approached the water with reverence, then all was lost as great sighs groaned from their throats and water flew in every direction. The bald man wet his turban and wound it back around his head, where it dripped steadily down his face.

Lili glanced around to see if she was alone. No one within hearing distance except the lunatic watering the mules and that didn't matter. She watched the Russians splash for a few moments and then her lips opened on their own and her voice said, Please—

We have these for you, Midhat interrupted from behind her, puffing from his jog. He thrust several towels into Lili's arms. You may give them the towels, he said grandly.

Numbness overwhelmed Lili as she stepped forward and they took the towels from her arms. If Midhat had not been here, she would have handed them the chains and the Russians would have been embracing her as a newly found compatriot, arranging for her protection and discussing their plans for departure.

So, that is better, said the bald one. He seemed to be their predesignated speaker, the other two Russians watched with their blunt eyes. Let's talk.

They walked back, footsteps lighter in the sand.

Yes, all in good time. First we must eat.

Nothing to eat, it is too hot.

Then tea. He called to Raja, Tea for our friends.

Hot tea? Never mind the tea.

Hot tea cools the soul. Try it.

Hot, too hot.

Nothing happens in the desert without a reason. Hot tea cools the soul.

Raja passed the tea around, keeping her telltale blue eyes to the ground. The Russians begrudgingly sipped at the tea and sweat some more.

This makes me hotter, said the bald man.

You should not shave your head in such heat, you have no protection from the sun.

My head was covered. And I didn't shave it.

Your mules are too slow.

They can carry more. And they're lower to the ground. Now, what about our business?

Perhaps one more cup of tea?

We don't want another damn cup of tea.

All right, first a toast.

A toast cannot be done without vodka.

I do not have vodka, but I have this. Midhat held up a clear bottle filled with a milky liquid.

Raja yelped and then remembered to cast her eyes down. It is forbidden, she murmured.

The silver-haired Russian examined the bottle. What is it?

Nectar of the gods. Palm wine.

Ouma snorted from within the tent. The Russians glanced at the tent and frowned.

What is wrong with it?

It can be a little strong, maybe too strong for you?

Too strong? the silver-haired Russian laughed, his laugh deep in his chest as if it had been suppressed in a bottle and let out with the pop of a cork. Never too strong, he said.

A peaceful breeze nipped through the air and the Russians smiled.

Pour us a toast, said the silver-haired man.

Yes, Midhat said as he carefully tipped the bottle so that a thin stream ran into a small glass. A toast.

Midhat passed the glasses to the Russians and said, To our business.

The Russians held up their shots. The bald man scowled and said, What about theirs?

They are my wives and they do not drink.

Everyone must drink with us.

It is against our religion.

You're drinking.

Midhat sighed and placed the palms of his hands together in front of him. When I was younger, I tasted the pork of a nonbeliever. Allah, forgive me, it was the best thing I had ever eaten and I couldn't stop. I felt no guilt, not as I savored the spicy forbidden meat or after. At that point, I knew my conscience would never play a part in my goodness.

The bald man set down his glass, folded his arms and said, I don't trust something here.

They will drink. We will all take a small drink. Midhat poured two more and handed one to Raja and one to Lili.

It's not vodka, the bald man said, but it will do.

He held his glass up and waited until everyone did the same. Nastravia, he said and tossed his head and glass back at the same time. Not vodka, he rasped.

Lili smelled the pungency of the alcohol as it neared her nose. Her eyes watered. She slid the glass under her veil and took a sip. She shuddered—too strong after weeks with no alcohol. Seconds later, Lili decided she liked the lift the palm wine gave her, sort of a gauzy, no-worries feeling. And although she was still hot, it didn't matter as much. She finished the rest in a single shot.

Midhat drew his eyebrows together and threw her an angry glance.

She drinks like a real Russian woman, said the silver-haired one. Be proud of her.

The third Russian, the one who never spoke, stood and started toward the mules. I have something your wife must try, he said.

Lili watched him leave, she would follow him in a moment. He was the perfect one to talk to, quiet, subdued, cowed. It made him seem vulnerable. Perhaps it was the innate instinct to attack the weakest.

Midhat's lips jumped. He turned to the two remaining Russians and cleared his throat. Have you heard of this woman in the desert?

The Russians glanced at each other. What sort of a woman?

The spirit of the desert.

Are you offering us a woman?

I cannot offer her, Midhat explained. It's your good luck if you see her.

We saw her.

Gabriel walked up and said, Aisha Qandisha is her name.

The bald man pointed at Gabriel and then the bottle. Midhat poured another glass.

We didn't know her name, but she has already offered herself to us.

Excuse me?

She is a jenni, a spirit, said Gabriel. She is said to be the most beautiful woman in the world.

We don't have such lunacy in Russia.

I am sorry for you.

When she appears, Gabriel continued, it is said she gives men all their hidden desires. Great treasures and bliss.

Midhat frowned at him. Gabriel stopped talking and smiled uncertainly.

It is all stories, said the Russian. These things do not exist. Arabian tales.

The desert is not like Russia. Things are different here.

Slowly Lili stood, retreated a few steps and then dashed through the sand to catch up with the third Russian.

Pazhalsta, she called, take me from here. Ya Russkiy.

He turned and stared at her with his flat eyes.

Look, Lili said and struggled to lift her robe over her head to show him her Russian whiteness and long Russian bones.

Whores, he said in Russian. Even in the middle of the desert you find us.

Lili stopped moving and choked. She yanked her robe back down.

Niet, ya . . . I'm not a whore, I'm Russian, one of your own. Don't you recognize me? You must help me. I can pay.

But Lili was frantic and her words came out in a jumble of Russian and Arabic and he laughed at her and turned away. She grabbed ahold of his sleeve and tugged on it, he shooed her away like a desert gnat.

Not now, he said.

She pulled out her bag and dangled it. I will give you this—

But Lili felt the lightness of the bag and when she shook it, it was obvious the chains were gone. She buckled into the sand and upended the bag—only rocks, desert rocks to give it weight and an empty bag.

30

Aisha

Am I Aisha Qandisha? Aisha, the beautiful jenni with feet of a goat, who dwells near water holes, rivers and baths. Aisha, the Moroccan siren who lures people to their doom, causes uncontrollable ecstasy and ultimately destructive obsession. Every Moroccan has heard of and fears Aisha Qandisha. The Arab was so fearful of her, he refused to call her by her name. He called her Lalla Aisha, as if to soften the risk of her power.

Is she the me who has lain dormant, ready to spring out and assert herself? Will I now possess lovers and destroy lives in my path? Is this the Lili I've feared?

At Madame Mer's, Rosa kissed me and fell recklessly in love. I see the kiss as an accident. It happened on our first and only outing to the beach. We stood clustered, unsure of what to do with the gritty sand and endless water. Under our robes, we wore our swimsuits, never to be seen on the beach itself. Not because of the sun, it was low in the sky, the palest trace of the sun's strength peeping over the horizon. Not because others weren't wearing bathing suits. It was because the men would not like others to feast their eyes on our bodies. We sat on the sand and splashed in the water covered by our damp robes.

Rosa ran to the water and dove in. We watched in admiration, her dives were beautiful. The others stood politely in the shallows, waiting for her to emerge, while I, who was familiar with the tricks of the ocean, ran to where she had disappeared. It was difficult to see through the churning waves, the swirling blanket of sand. A hand appeared as if it were beckoning me to join it in the water. I grabbed the hand and pulled until the rest of Rosa emerged, dazed and waterlogged.

Rosa had never seen the ocean snatch back the water from the shore, she didn't expect the water to fight her. We had all been taught to resuscitate someone, but no one wanted to touch lips with poor Rosa. So I did. I put my lips to hers and blew. Before long she was sucking the air out of me rather than my blowing it into her. That kiss was an accident.

Madame Mer heard about the infatuation and separated us. Rosa stopped speaking. Madame Mer claimed she was possessed by Aisha Qandisha. A member of the Hamasha was brought in to break the spell, an old man who arrived with some musicians and danced around, before falling into a trace. Rosa was declared cured. No one heard her speak again and two weeks later she was taken away to her new husband.

And the Arab, what about him? Did I cause his demise? Is Raja right in saying Gabriel has been possessed by Aisha? His passion is out of control. He is helpless to his infatuation and perhaps only when Aisha releases him will he have his own resolve back. Is Aisha me? Have I caused this?

I withdraw a leg from under my robe, examining it carefully. My leg has a light covering of hair, as I have nothing to shave with. My fine little feet are hard and dark with gnarled spots and chipped toenails with black cracks. Surely this does not constitute hooves? Does it? Am I Aisha?

31

Plan Deux

THE SEARING SAND BURNED LILI'S LEGS THROUGH HER DJELLABA, but she didn't care. With the chains gone, her chances were gone. She would have to remain at this murky hole in the desert. She turned the pouch inside out to make sure it was empty. It was. A tear dropped from her eye and fell on the rocks, evaporating as soon as it landed. Mixed in with the rocks was a folded scrap of paper. Lili opened it and found inside several tiny worms, they looked dead.

She peered closer, prodding them with her fingernail. They were not worms at all, they were thick black hairs. Panic rushed up from her stomach and clenched her chest. The Arab's hairs, the same hairs she had buried in the sand long ago. Had someone dug them up, stolen her chains and switched the gold for the hair?

A sob pushed from her chest and she threw herself down, burying her face, drowning herself in the sand the same way she had tried to drown herself in the ocean her first week with the Arab. He had taken her to a beautiful beach, Essouria. She had walked straight into the water and cried. Great, muted wails that were carried up in bubbles to break on the surface. She never knew if he heard the explosions of sound on the surface as they broke.

Lili inhaled the sand, granules scraping her face, flowing into her mouth, she chewed them between her teeth, grinding and grinding until she was deafened by the noise.

Someone slid his hands under her armpits and gently lifted her up. Her mind had come to a stop, no more thoughts or plans or ideas existed inside her. The lunatic's eyes appeared before her. He softly swept a finger across her face, brushing away the grains of sand. She stared past the lunatic at the blank desert. No eye contact, no eye contact, she repeated to herself in a mantra. No eye contact.

She exhaled and coughed. Sand sputtered from her lips and nose. She sneezed, her eyes ran, her lungs felt raw. She spat mouthful after mouthful of sand onto the ground. He shook her a few times, placing her upright on her feet. He took a firm hold of her upper arm and pulled her behind him. She staggered after him, relieved to have someone taking charge of her life. He pushed her down into the bushes and they crouched there near the mules, doing nothing.

She stared at the gray, dusty leaves in front of her. Grit scratched her eyes and they watered in pain. She wet the tip of her finger with her tears and washed off one of the leaves. Underneath it shone a strong green.

Gradually, the Russians' voices broke through her inertia and she felt hatred. Hard, chest-squeezing hatred. It put a spark back into Lili's heart. From the corner of her eye, she saw that the lunatic had his ear turned toward the Russians and then she grasped that he wanted her to eavesdrop on their conversation.

The silver-haired man had joined the other and as he rummaged in his bags for something, they talked in low voices.

—be enough?

—village is small. They will fear us. The silver-haired one laughed his deep laugh.

—hate us.

They already hate us.

—punish them for destroying the mines—

There was another whore—

—blue eyes?

Nah.

These women are either whores or saints.

Lili looked at the lunatic to see if he understood. He looked at her to see if she understood. It was a mistake, the eye contact, a release button triggered and they fell upon each other with a ferocity that knocked them to the ground and gnashed their teeth together. Distantly, on some other plane in her mind, Lili heard the deep laugh again and looked up through the bushes, around the lunatic's robe, to see the Russians watching them.

There she is, there's the whore.

Lili returned to the tents, the hatred still hard in her heart. A finger stuck out of Ouma's tent and motioned desperately to Lili. One of Ouma's eyes peeped out of an open seam. Lili stopped at the back of the tent and crouched down next to Ouma's dark kohled eye.

I lied to you, Ouma said. Where have you been?

You took my chains.

You've been drinking, Ouma smiled.

Yes. What about my chains?

Chains to what?

I had three gold chains and they are gone. Someone at the oasis stole them.

We don't steal at this oasis. She caught Lili's expression and added, At least not from each other.

We don't steal from each other and we don't lie to each other, is that what you're telling me?

I was looking for you.

What did you lie about?

I want the arms myself. That is the true reason I agreed to help Midhat, not what I told you.

You?

They have killed my lover. The Russians. I am sure.

Why would they do that?

I was the connection, she whispered, to the rebels. My lover sold the rebels the arms. He believed in them, in their cause. He was a saint.

Ouma pounded the tent wall with a fist.

Midhat only wanted the money. My lover never told him I was involved, although Midhat suspects. There was already an agreement
that those arms would be sold to the rebels, not to the Russians.

What do the rebels want with weapons?

Ouma's eye looked out desperately. We need them.

Nobody needs them.

How are my people to get out of the camps?

They are already in the camps. What will arms do for them?

There is a plan.

Lili thought about telling Ouma of the Russians' plan to terrorize
the village, but Ouma's intensity made her keep silent. It was a circle. Either the Russians use the weapons to kill the villagers or the
rebels use the weapons to kill the Russians. Both of them fighting
for the wealth under this sea of sand. Neither of them should have
the arms.

I don't want to kill anyone else, Lili said.

Who has been killed? What do you know about my lover?

No, I know nothing about your lover. I am sure he is alive, I just
don't want anyone to die.

No one will die. It is a perfect plan. Ouma shook her head, the eye
disappearing and reappearing several times. You don't understand. It
is for the desert rally.

Rally?

Race cars.

They're going to kill race-car drivers?

No killing, only warning. They are driving through a war zone.

Here?

Yes, the desert.

Everything is so bewildering here, Lili said.

Yes, Ouma sighed. They need to bring attention to themselves, so
people don't forget what is happening. They will blow up the road.
She caught sight of Lili's face. Not with anyone on it.

I will help steal the arms back, but not to give them to the rebels.
No deaths. They cannot be trusted.

Lili couldn't organize her thoughts in a straight line. They floated randomly inside her head and just as she thought she had a grip on one idea, it would swerve away. She thought the best way to deal with the arms would be to get rid of them, so that no one had access to them.

We will get rid of the mines ourselves, Lili said. No one will have them but us.

Ouma's eye grew big. What about the rebels?

Too risky. We will blow up the land mines ourselves.

Ouma's eye widened even bigger. Us? If we're going to blow them up, we might as well blow them up on the road. That way we can make sure no one is around.

Lili considered the idea. Okay. She squinted suspiciously at Ouma. Don't you have to discuss it with anyone? The leaders?

No.

Why not?

Ouma's eye roved around Lili's face, finally resting on her left cheekbone. You are talking to them.

You? You are in charge of the rebels?

There are few rebels here anymore.

The rebels? You?

The rebels are now either refugees or they have disappeared. Poof. Gone. Where did they go?

Where could they go? Morocco to the north, Mauritania to the south, Atlantic Ocean to the west—they could only go east to Algeria, over the border. That or die.

You were going to blow up the land mines by yourself?

Ouma met Lili's eyes. Yes.

Oh, Ouma. Lili imagined petite Ouma sneaking into the middle of the desert, lugging a supply of arms, setting them up and blowing the road to pieces as she danced a jig. Ouma leading her one-woman rebellion.

I knew you were sent to help me. Didn't I tell you that? For now I will be nice to the Russian bastards and then we will rob them. I hate them so much you wouldn't believe.

I believe.

The bald Russian was pouring another round of vodka. Lili held her head high as she walked back into the center of the camp. If these men were a representation of what people were like in Russia, she wanted nothing to do with Russia. They were no better than the gypsies who had rejected her and she looked forward to robbing them. Bastards.

Ouma sashayed out of the tent, a veil across her face, tied so high her heavy kohl-rimmed eyes barely peered above. She stopped next to the Russians and held out a platter of dates. Lili could see her narrowed eyes as she stooped next to the silver-haired man. She wondered if Ouma were poisoning them. He popped two dates into his mouth. Lili closed her eyes and waited for him to go blind.

Ouma picked up an empty glass and held it out to Midhat. He eyed Ouma nervously. He shook his head. She cleared her throat and stood directly in front of him.

No, he said.

The Russian stomped his foot on the sand. All the women will drink.

Of course.

Midhat poured Ouma a small serving. He held up his glass. To our guests, nastravia.

Ouma held up her glass and looked over the top of her veil at Lili. To the Russians, she said.

Lili smiled and held her glass up to the toast. Yes, to the Russians.

Everyone drank except for the silver-haired one, who scowled and asked, Why to the Russians?

It must be difficult being Russian, Ouma said. Russians are always the bad guys.

Excuse me, Midhat caught Ouma's arm and pinched her. Very disobedient wife.

They looked at Ouma with interest and the bald one started to pour another shot into her glass.

One is enough for the ladies, Midhat said.

Well, why don't we ask them?

Ouma said to Midhat, If we are taking a holiday from being Muslim today, it might as well be a good one.

She thrust her glass out to the Russian.

The Russian poured in a generous amount and looked around.

And your wife, the one with the Russian traits. He threw his head back and laughed and poured Lili another hefty measure.

A wave of hatred swept over Lili, leaving her breathless. Russian traits will never make a Russian, she spat out.

Midhat clamped a hand on Lili's shoulder. Ignore these women, the heat, it swells their brains.

Raja stared at the ground and shook her head when the Russian tried to pour more into her glass, but he ignored her and filled it until it overflowed. Nastravia, he shouted. What about dancing girls?

No, no dancing girls here, only my wives.

Can't they dance? What about that one? He looked at Ouma. She seems lively.

No. Definitely not, she has a lame leg. But he can dance, Midhat pointed to Gabriel. Dance, Gabriel, dance.

I can dance.

Gabriel kicked his feet a few times and started clapping rapidly. Once he had a rhythm, he started snapping his fingers and clicking his toes. The Russians were impressed and called for more shots all around.

Nastravia!

Gabriel leaped in a circle, whirled over to Raja and yanked her to her feet. He planted her limbs in the proper positions and they were off, twirling and dipping. Raja giggled nervously, clutching on to her veil with one hand. Two more dips and she was whooping, her laugh floating up into the afternoon sky. Midhat scurried after them and tried to step in between, but they moved too quickly and he looked ridiculous chasing them round and round.

The bald Russian slapped Midhat on the back. Midhat, I had doubts about you, but you give a good party. Drinking, dancing, women, what more can a Russian ask for? Now, the vodka is gone and it is time for serious talk.

The palm wine, we haven't finished the palm wine.

Where are the arms?

What is the hurry?

What are you up to? You promised us arms, you said, "enough arms to blow the Sahara to the heavens." Those were your exact words.

I . . .

Now, where are they?

We are a two-dozen-tree oasis, have pity on us.

I don't care if you are a one-tree oasis. I knew we shouldn't have trusted you. You promised us something and we want it.

The sandstorm has buried everything and I cannot find it. Buried under a mound, but which mound?

He's lying.

Fuck your mother. The third one leaned menacingly toward Midhat. Get the arms.

Midhat scurried to his tent and reappeared dragging a wooden box.

Good, good, said the bald one. Where's the rest?

It's . . . this is it.

What do you mean, this is it? He turned his head sideways and read the box. Land mines. Fine. Put them near the mules, he directed the third Russian. He turned back to Midhat.

I repeat, "enough arms to blow the Sahara to the heavens." Now, where are they?

Midhat wrung his hands, twitched his chin and said nothing.

Stand up, you fat Cossack, the bald one said, looking at the silver-haired man. This man is tricking us.

The silver-haired Russian stood up, wobbling on his feet. Where are the arms?

Something is fucked up. The third man returned and held his head in his hands, blinking rapidly. I don't feel right. You bastard, you've drugged us. Vodka doesn't make me feel like this.

No, no drugs. The heat. Tea and vodka. Palm wine. Not a good combination.

He's lying again.

You will regret this. The bald man stumbled to his feet.

I am an honorable man.

We were going to pay for the arms, but because you lied to us, we're not.

He lurched at Midhat and grabbed his arms, pinning them behind his back.

Oh, Midhat, you really shouldn't have done that.

He struggled to free his arms. What?

Lied to us.

I am innocent.

The silver-haired man found a rope and they knotted one end first around Midhat's wrists and then his ankles.

Stop standing around gawking, Midhat shouted. Help me, one of you idiots, help me!

The Russians carried him over to the tallest date tree and dropped him underneath in the dust. The bald man threw the free end of the rope up into the air and over a frond of the date tree.

Raja, I am your husband, you must help me. I order you to help me. I will divorce you, I swear.

Raja raised a hand toward Midhat. Her hand fluttered uncertainly before she slowly lowered it. She looked at Gabriel. The Russians took the end of the rope and pulled and pulled until Midhat was hauled feet first into the air. Strung up like a slaughtered lamb.

Raja, Raja, what have I done to you? Help me.

The date tree shuddered. Midhat's turban slipped and uncoiled slowly into the sand. The Russians nodded, satisfied, at Midhat.

Swing him, the silver-haired Russian said.

The other two grabbed his shoulders, pulled him way back and let go. Midhat swung toward the palm tree, bumping his shoulder and cursing like a heathen. A gun appeared from the boot of the silver-haired man. He leveled it at Midhat as Midhat dangled and swayed from the tree. *Bang*. He took one shot and there was a splash in the water. *Bang*, another shot and bark flew off the tree.

Look, Gabriel called out and pointed to the Russians' mules. Look.

The mules were untethered and slowly walking off into the desert. Saddleless, riderless and armsless.

Motherfucker, shouted the quiet Russian.

He and the bald one ran after the mules, leaving the third Russian behind. As the two men approached the mules, the beasts picked up speed and jogged away. The silver-haired Russian looked at his comrades. He looked back at Midhat dangling from the tree and then back at the mules.

Scheet, he muttered and ran to join in the chase.

Oh merciful Allah, cried Raja. They've taken the money and the arms. All is lost.

All is not lost. Get me down from here, now.

Gabriel slashed the rope with a knife and Midhat tumbled down in an undignified heap. He wiggled his feet.

Pins and needles, pins and needles. After all I've done for you, sacrificed my toes, saved your lives . . .

Midhat, you lied, said Raja.

Not to you. Never to you.

You lied to them.

Them? The Russians? Who cares about them? We've got them where we want them, in the desert with all their money.

Gabriel extended his arm and pointed at the Russians who were busy saddling their mules. They're stealing your arms.

We steal them back. That was the idea.

They have guns.

We'll steal them, too.

This is too dangerous, said Gabriel. Let the Russians have the weapons.

And you lied. Raja's face was pale.

My sweet cup of tea, my rose petal, I would never lie to you. And Raja, what about my plan?

Raja lowered her eyes.

You, I will never lie to. Never. And as your husband, I demand you obey me.

Lili thought about Ouma's son and the little girl with the yellow flower and how the red walls of the village would explode into a shower of dirt. We have to take back the weapons, she said.

Midhat's face went through a series of contortions ranging from in-credulous to untrusting. Ouma nodded in agreement.

Lili continued, I've heard what they are going to do with them.

Ouma gasped and spun Lili around so they faced each other. What? she hissed. You cannot tell them.

Ouma, I heard them talking. The Russians, not the rebels.

You said nothing to me.

What exactly did you hear? Gabriel asked.

Lili turned back to the group. They are going to destroy Ouma's village.

Allah have mercy. My son. Why would they do such a thing?

They think the village is behind the attacks on their mines.

Maybe they are, Midhat said.

No, Ouma said, not the village. No one in the village is involved.

Well . . .

I am sure. Sure because I was chased from the village to ensure everyone's safety. That's how sure. And that's how I knew my husband could not want me back. It would be too dangerous for everyone.

I knew it. I knew it! Midhat slapped the palm of his hand with his fist. You were the connection. You conniving bitch. I knew I should have chased you away.

Look. Gabriel pointed into the desert. There they go.

The Russians had strapped the arms onto a mule and were leaving.

Quick, Midhat said. On with our plan. Hurry. Lili will entice the Russians with her beauty and song, she will be dressed as Aisha Qan-disha. A Saharan siren. He looked at Lili skeptically.

Lipstick, makeup, comb, water, shine . . . quick, quick. Everyone must help. Lili, put on your gold dress and meet in Fatima's tent. Run, run.

Lili rushed to her tent and found the gold dress. She gave it a good shake, the silk rustled, puffs of dust rose into the air. It was still in fairly good condition, if she ignored the small tears and missing se-quins. The luxurious fabric whispered over her skin. Although she had only been wearing the djellaba for several weeks, she felt naked in her gown. She ran to Fatima's tent.

They were waiting for her. She sat in the middle of the tent. Midhat made her sit down in the middle of the rug. Gabriel dipped his fingertips into a cup of oil and massaged it into her scalp. He ran a blunt-edged comb through her hair until it splayed onto her shoulders in a shining cascade.

Ouma quickly ground some kohl into a fine powder. She added a few drops of water and dipped a polished rock the size of a pencil into the kohl. With a steady hand she traced the outline of Lili's eyes.

Lili had the distressing sensation that she was being prepared for sacrifice. She tried to catch Ouma's eyes, but Ouma only bit her lip and snapped, Stop moving.

Raja sprinkled Lili's arms with fake gold dust and rubbed it in with oil until a bronze glow appeared on her skin. She dampened a brown powder and brushed it on her lips. Fatima stood near the doorway listening and sniffing the air.

They finished and stepped back, staring at Lili. She stared back at them, uneasy.

Look, Raja said and she held up a small mirror for Lili to look into.

Lili gazed at the reflection and shrank back, sickened by the sight in the mirror. It was the Arab's visor again and this time she didn't recognize herself, this garish woman with over-accented eyes and melting red mouth.

Madame Mer had told her girls that beauty needs contrasts. If you don't know something exists, how can you know about the opposite? "Keep something ugly around," she said to her girls. "The best is an ugly friend. She will show what you are not." Lili caught another glimpse of her tawdry face in the mirror. She was the ugly friend.

These men were on mules, Midhat said. We will take the long way around on the camels and surprise them by the rocks. Enshallah. Mules are slow, we can easily catch them.

Surprise them and what? Gabriel asked.

Do you have a better suggestion?

What will we surprise them with?

Lili.

Me?

You will divert the Russians with your lullaby. You will be a magnet. You will be Aisha Qandisha, luring men to their destiny.

I won't. Why me? Why can't Ouma do this?

They may recognize her.

Raja?

She's my wife.

Lili eyed Gabriel. He shook his head.

You said yourself that we have to get the arms back, Midhat said. Everyone will contribute, like we discussed, enshallah. You will sing, Gabriel, with his dune knowledge, will bury us—

Bury us? Ouma said.

Hide us in the dunes. Disguise the mounds of sand so they look like real dunes and the Russians cannot see us. Fatima will wail and frighten them.

And me? Raja asked.

You are to help capture the Russians.

Raja's eyes grew and grew until the whites showed. She blushed. I cannot.

I order you to.

I am not strong, I am not a man.

I have seen you carry buckets of water. You are as strong as a mule. Why does everyone challenge me? Disobedient and ungrateful women surround me.

The lunatic had the camels saddled and ready. Midhat led the way into the desert. Not long after they started, Midhat turned off the path and galloped his camel up a huge sloping dune, everyone following, Lili holding on to the awkward saddle and gritting her teeth so hard she felt sure one of them would snap. The camels lunged up and down the dunes, sand spraying out from their huge feet. Eventually, the group came upon a bed of large rocks. They walked the camels across. On the other side of the rocks, they found the path.

Lili, you will stand on those rocks back there. We will wait here, and when they approach, we jump out and rob them.

It sounds so easy. Gabriel looked frightened.

It is easy, Midhat said. Push the sand up to form a mound and crouch behind it, so it looks like a dune. Gabriel will arrange them to look real. Remember, no talking around the Russians. They must believe we are desert bandits.

We are desert bandits.

Raja, Midhat turned to her and fixed her with a look. Take Fatima to those rocks and make sure she is hidden. Fatima, you will begin to wail after you hear Lili sing and just as we surprise the Russians, enshallah. Not before. You must listen carefully.

I can only listen carefully.

Maybe the Russians have already passed by, said Gabriel.

Not on those mules. But hurry.

Gabriel smoothed the dunes sideways with a long stick, taking care to sweep the sand in the direction of the wind. Raja crouched behind her mound and peered over at Lili. She threw something at Lili's feet, the green-feathered charm.

Green is the color of Allah. Take this with you, for protection.

Lili held up the charm and looked at it. Sunlight shot through the green feathers with an eerie glow. She couldn't imagine a bird so brilliant. She handed it back to Raja.

It's dead.

It's still a charm.

This can't bring good luck. You killed the bird for these feathers, Raja. Do you want this to be me?

Look what it has done for me. She patted her stomach.

Enshallah, Lili said and then caught herself. But she wasn't Muslim anymore. She had nothing against being a Muslim, it was just that she was told to be one, even though she wasn't. She drank, never prayed or visited a mosque, didn't give alms to the poor and had never been to Mecca. Not a very good Muslim.

She wasn't sure what she thought about Allah or any other god, for that matter. She was no longer the girl Madame Mer created or the wife the Arab required her to be. Someone had certainly made her life a mess and if it was God who was responsible, she didn't think highly of him.

Then Lili prayed anyway. Not to Allah, but to something less tangible, not a being or a creature. More of a presence inside herself. She prayed to not be killed: I promise I will not lie, cheat, or steal, if I live. She couldn't think of any more sins she should not commit. And any I think of later, she added.

Gabriel finished with the dunes. He erased the footsteps one at a time before burying himself and smoothing over his own mound.

Ready, he called.

Lili tied the charm around her neck and trudged through the sand toward the rocks. Her mind felt flat and lethargic. Her life was unrecognizable. She was stuck in the desert, about to sing lullabies to three Russians that she would rob and then she would help blow up a road. She was robbing her own people. Despicable as they were, they were still her people. Or were they? Maybe she was more of a gypsy, belonging nowhere and to no one.

Abandoned among the rocks sat a convertible Volkswagen Beetle with a rental car sticker on the bumper. Several sun-bleached champagne bottles lay in the backseat. A few tatters of clothing were discarded in the sand. Lili stood on the wreckage to get more height and opened her arms wide to catch the trace of a delicate breeze.

Moments later, just as Midhat said, the mules came plodding into sight, the Russians unsteady on their backs. At the sight of the Russians, her dullness lifted and hatred sparkled into her body. The shoot of yellow-green life pulsed in her center.

She hummed softly first, then louder until words took shape and she broke gently into song. The mules saw her first. They stiffened their legs and craned their necks, pointing their ears in her direction. The bald man in the lead whipped his head around, stared at Lili, turned back and slowly turned around again. He reined in his mule and everything behind him came to a halt. The group stood motionless. The feathers around Lili's neck rustled in the breeze. She took them off and threw them high into the sky, where they caught a whirlwind and spun up and up with the gauzy dust.

Lili sang with more strength, she felt wonderful. The green sprout grew. The line of mules moved in her direction, slowly as if in a trance. She was a magnet. She was Aisha Qandisha.

The bald man spoke first as they approached her. It's an angel.

It's a whore.

It's the devil.

They stared at Lili's platform.

Look what happened to the last people. He pointed to the abandoned convertible.

They were almost to the correct position when Fatima began to wail. Midhat let out a muffled curse. The Russians spun around and stared wildly behind them. Mounds of sand exploded and Midhat, Gabriel, Raja and Ouma burst out of their piles.

Bandits, robbers.

Lord help us.

The mules bolted. Two of the Russians immediately lost their balance and tumbled off the mules. The bald Russian held precariously to the mane of his mule as it ran into the desert. Strapped to the back was the box of land mines, bouncing up and down.

Lili's voice swelled, the green shoot grew more and more powerful.

They tied the Russians' hands together and unloaded the mules. Midhat went through the Russians' pockets and sacks, shoving wads of money and pieces of gold into his own bag.

A figure appeared around the rocks. The lunatic leading the runaway mule with the arms and the third Russian draped over the back like a sack of chickpeas.

Gabriel cut the box of land mines from the mule and carefully set it on the ground. They hoisted the two remaining Russians frontways over their mules and tied them on.

When all three Russians were lying over the backs of the mules, Midhat grinned and took out his knife. He approached the silver-haired man from behind. The other two Russians widened their eyes and began gibbering in Russian. In one quick slash, Midhat cut through the material of the Russian's trousers, the ripping noise loud in the quiet desert. His white buttocks gleamed in the sunlight. The bald Russian sobbed.

Midhat did the same with the other two and whacked the mules across their hind legs with a strap of leather. They darted off straight into the desert.

It is only fitting that they have as much humiliation as they have given me, Midhat said. He chortled. They won't be able to sit for weeks.

What if the mules head off into the middle of the desert and they die? asked Gabriel. You will have three deaths on your hands.

A mule may be thick in the head, but it's not so stupid that it will run away from water and food and its home.

Ouma tugged on the hem of Lili's dress. You can stop singing now.

But Lili couldn't stop. The green bloom had blossomed into a flower. Her mouth kept opening and closing, the notes swirling around her in dizzy tornadoes.

32

Caza

Caza was everything the desert is not. Caza meant a place teeming with people, gasping in the lugubrious air, gulping whiskey and Cokes, surrounded by a cacophony of horns and the roar of air conditioning . . . and in the desert nothing. I was not prepared for the nothingness. The silence.

Silence is a thought I cannot empty from my head. It invades me, pushes against my inner skin. A birdcall, a camel roar, makes the silence take flight for a second, but it lands again. And the persisting wind is only another form of silence, blocking all vision and sight.

The clamor of silence obstructs my past, my life in Caza, the specifics of my relationship with the Arab. It wasn't real and it wasn't me. No one ever asked me what I thought and if I injected an opinion, they looked at me as if I'd belched. All they wanted was regurgitation of their own ideas. Mental masturbation. From me a muteness of self. All this time, through all this numbness, there existed a tiny sprout within a hard case that cracked as soon as the Arab was bitten by the snake.

My new reality is me, leaving tidbits of memories, party crumbs floating around my mind.

I am insanely jealous of Ouma and her lover, of their consuming affair, her dedication, her respect. I want what she has.

After Russia, all I ever wanted was to not want. I spent years not wanting, but I am awake now, and I want. I want an ardent lover, I want a life where I make decisions, I want to be my own person. Not the Arab's. Not Madame Mer's. The silence has provoked these wants.

The noise of civilization can smother anyone. It used to be that the Arab and his world were so big, so heavy, they surrounded me until all I had left was that tiny sprout deep inside. The desert has nurtured that sprout. I can see how small my world was. I can expand.

33

Snakeskin

THE NEXT DAY, LILI FELT REFRESHED, REJUVENATED AFTER ROBBING the Russians. Everyone at the oasis was buoyant. They had the arms and they had the money. The sun seemed less brutal, the sky smaller, the thorn bushes more friendly.

Lili sat upwind from the camels, cross-legged on the ground, next to Raja, who had consented to a private conversation with Gabriel, monitored by Lili. Lili could see straight down the path if anyone were approaching from the oasis and Gabriel was late. A palm tree rustled above them, a small bird dove and swooped around them trying to frighten them away.

Fatima wants to talk to you, said Raja.

What about?

Not only you, all of us. Except Midhat. Raja cleared her throat and looked off into the desert. It was me, Lili.

You what?

I stole your chains.

You?

So you didn't know? I tiptoed into your room, careful to be as quiet as the night, and replaced them with rocks while you slept. I am a better thief than I ever thought.

But why?

I didn't want you to leave and I knew there was something in that bag that would allow you to leave. I was right.

You couldn't have known.

I had a vision of you, I'm sure it was you, a gold angel, flying above the desert—away. Like the green bird tried to fly away.

Raja . . . where are my chains?

I don't know. They were taken from me.

Who took them from you?

Raja shrugged.

Gabriel ran up the path sweating and holding something in his left hand. A discarded snakeskin. He gave a neat bow before sitting next to Lili. He rolled the snakeskin between his fingers, glancing at Raja from the corner of his eyes. Raja sat immobile.

A snake can live without its skin, but I cannot, Gabriel burst out. He shook the snakeskin at Raja. You are under my skin. Have pity on me.

Raja stared at the ground. The only indication that she heard Gabriel's words was the sudden exhale that fluttered her veil.

It is your doing, Gabriel cried. Raja, you came to me, you put me under your spell.

She told me to. Raja threw Lili a sharp glance, a sliver of blue.

You? Gabriel turned to Lili. Why have you made my life so miserable?

I didn't . . . it wasn't meant in that way. It was a misunderstanding. All of it.

There is no misunderstanding here, I want Raja to leave Midhat and come to Spain with me. I will take care of her and the child. There can be no misunderstanding about that.

Raja gasped. Child? What do you know about a child?

She cast a bitter look at Lili. Lili studied the pathway with intense interest.

It is my child.

Stop. It is Midhat's child. There is no doubt.

Gabriel picked at the snakeskin, bit by bit shredding it into pieces that floated onto the sand. I cannot live without my skin any more than I can live without you. You must see this. Midhat doesn't treat you well, he has no respect for you, he . . .

I will hear no more about Midhat.

Midhat is not who you think he is.

How do you know who I think he is?

Because you could never love such a man, over me.

I will never leave him. You don't know him. It would take a miracle for me to leave Midhat. Do you believe in miracles?

Gabriel sat very still for a moment. In October 1987, small pink frogs dropped out of the sky in England, all the way from the Sahara. Is that a miracle?

You just don't know. You who sit in the desert all day digging and poking at the dunes looking for your stupid silver mine.

Mine? Lili asked. Not mind?

Silver mine.

Lili started laughing. Silver mine. I thought you were searching for your mind and you were crazy.

He is crazy, Raja said. Obsessed by Aisha Qandisha.

I'm sorry, said Lili.

It doesn't matter, Gabriel said. There was no mine, anyway.

Raja frowned at him. You lied. Why does everyone lie? I can't stand it.

There were no lies. I was looking for mines. Not silver mines, land mines that the terrorists planted.

What about the paper from your father?

Gabriel shook his head. That was a receipt for a watch.

You lied to me.

That was a small lie to support what everyone thought anyway. Everyone lies.

I hate liars.

Then you hate Midhat, too.

He has not lied to me.

He will.

Never. Never!

I had a good reason for my small lies and I'll tell you why, but only because I'm leaving the desert soon. I was watching Midhat.

Not very interesting, Raja sniffed.

On the contrary.

Why?

For the Spanish government. We suspected Midhat knew where the terrorists had planted the land mines.

You're a spy, Lili stated.

Raja sat with her back pointing to the heavens and looked him straight in the eyes, all the blueness focusing on Gabriel. Then why are you leaving? she asked.

Gabriel couldn't answer, he was hypnotized. Lili leaned forward and clapped her hands in front of his face.

He started and smiled at her. Nothing more to watch, he said. Midhat is here, but his connection has disappeared.

He has disappeared? Lili said. Ouma's lover?

Ouma's lover? Who is that?

No one. No one.

Raja was silent for a long time, staring at the oasis. She dug her fists into the fine sand and let it fall out in a stream. Have you ever seen a waterfall?

Gabriel blinked and said, yes.

How does it work?

Gabriel thought for a moment. It . . . runs over. And over.

But where does so much water come from?

The sky.

Raja looked up at the white-hot sky. I would like to see a waterfall. I will show you dozens of waterfalls.

No. Raja threw a handful of sand at Gabriel and ran down the path to the oasis.

You know she's mad, Lili said.

No, it's the desert, it does this to people. She will be fine outside the desert.

Everyone, except Midhat, stood shifting in the gloom of Fatima's tent. Fatima sat stiffly on the edge of her bed, all but disappearing into the darkness with her black robe and veil. The safety pins glinted dully.

Men are simple creatures, Fatima began. You only need to listen to them and you will know. Listen to what you hear, but do not believe all that is told.

I did not come here to be insulted, said Gabriel.

Listen to me. Midhat does not plan to share the wealth with any of you.

Midhat believes in the people of the desert, Raja said.

Midhat cares about how many dirhams cross his palms.

And us? Ouma asked. Our dreams? We were part of the plan.

You were not listening to him. It is his dreams that will come true. If you don't believe me, look at his toes. He's lied about those, too.

His toes are there? His toes are whole? All of them? All ten?

They are intact.

Midhat would never do that to us, Raja said. I refuse to be a part of this.

Raja, if we don't look, we will never know.

I don't believe you, Fatima. Anyway, why would you tell us if you did know something?

He will leave me behind, so I must tell you his plan.

Leave you behind? Asked Raja.

He is going away. Without a worry, he is leaving me, his first wife, behind. Even blind, I watch. He will take all the money you have gathered and go.

Go? . . . Go where?

To start a new life. To buy new wives.

He will steal from us all that we have stolen?

You must believe me. Look at his toes. You can stop him and he will have to stay here, but I want all of you to leave if I tell you where he hid the money.

Not me, Raja said. He's my husband, too.

All of you must go.

Never. You've been plotting to get rid of me since I arrived. I won't leave.

Tell him you want your portion of the money and see what he says.

My portion is his portion. And he would never leave me, not Midhat and not after I'm pregnant with his child.

He doesn't believe you are pregnant.

Why wouldn't he believe me?

He thinks you are lying.

I don't lie.

But he does, and when someone is a liar that person thinks everyone else is a liar. He thinks you don't want to be sent back to your
village. Look at his toes.

Lili sat silent thinking about this possibility, picturing his brown
toes all lined up along the top of his unscarred foot.

He wouldn't lie to me, Raja whispered.

We need to know, said Ouma.

Ouma stealthily untied the leather strips holding Midhat's tent door
closed, stopping every few seconds to listen for a noise. She crawled
inside, Lili behind, and they saw Midhat lying on his stomach, snor-
ing loudly. A thin cotton sheet twisted around his body.

We have to make him turn over, Ouma whispered.

Lili pinched his ankle as if an ant had bitten it. He grunted and
flopped over like an egg in a pan. She smiled. A slash of sunlight
came through the tent door falling on the two bumps that were Midhat's feet. Ouma picked up the sheet with two fingers and slowly,
slowly lifted it and uncovered one foot. Five toes. Slowly to the other
and . . . callused and dirty with opaque nails curving upward . . . another five toes. Ten whole toes. Not one of them bruised.

Give me your bra, Ouma said to Lili.

What?

Ouma struggled with her bra under her robe for a few moments
and then quickly tied it around Midhat's ankles. Midhat woke up and
roared. He saw Ouma and Lili crouched next to him, Lili struggling
under her robe.

How dare you wake me.

How dare you lie to us.

Lie? Get out of my tent. I didn't invite you here, he bellowed. Out. Now.

He stood up and promptly fell forward onto the floor, face first. Ouma and Lili pounced on him and tied his wrists behind his back with Lili's bra. He roared again. From outside the tent, there was a high-pitched whimpering.

Who is that? Untie me.

Lili opened the tent door and Raja lay outside curled into a ball, sobbing. Midhat's head faced the door and he found himself staring at Raja, floor level.

What's wrong with you? Help me.

You lied. Raja began throwing handfuls of sand in Midhat's face. You lied to me.

Midhat clenched his eyes shut. Never, I wouldn't. Raja, stop this. Get these two lunatics away from me.

She continued throwing the sand. You lied.

Ouma held up one of his shoes and whacked it against the tent pole. Several rocks fell out of the front. What about your toes? Ouma asked. How did they grow back?

Midhat stopped struggling. My toes, they were for fun. Sometimes people need a little motivating and that's what they were, motivators.

Where's the money?

What money?

I want my share of the money right now.

Girls, untie me and we can discuss this properly.

Where are the land mines?

What do you want with the land mines?

Lili and Ouma looked at each other and they shrugged.

I know what you're up to, he said. The rally. You girls are crazy, it has already passed. The cars went by yesterday. Didn't you hear them?

No, Ouma shook her head. It's not possible. The cars do not pass until tomorrow morning.

Maybe he's right, Lili said.

Midhat strained at the binding. Let me go and I'll help you.

You said the rally passed.

Yes—

Don't believe him. He's a liar. Ouma jumped up. When has he ever spoken the truth to us?

Stupid fools, you'll kill yourselves.

Raja lay on the ground with her head pressed to the sand. I am the stupid fool, she said. All this time, I was not using my eyes to see. I was blinder than Fatima. You were going to leave me? Your pregnant wife in the middle of the desert. I thought all you wanted was your son.

I do, I do.

You lied about lying to me.

Gabriel peered through the doorway, his bright eyes taking in Midhat prone on the floor, his hands tied and Raja wilted in the sand.

Raja, untie me, so we can be together. We have a life together . . . our son . . . please.

Snake. Gabriel was right. You are an evil snake trying to shed Fatima and me. And I hate you.

Gabriel smiled and ducked back outside. Ouma gazed around the room. She kicked the mattress over and pushed over a pile of blankets. Lili lifted a rug and peered underneath. She tossed the first rug aside and pulled up another. The box of land mines was dug into the earth so that it was flat.

Here, Lili called to Ouma. Here they are, next to the bed.

All right, now where's the money?

No money, Midhat groaned.

Ouma cut open his mattress and ripped out the straw in fierce fistfuls. Lili opened a chest and tossed out each piece of clothing separately.

Tell us where.

I won't say.

Lili stepped closer. Without that money and her chains, she had nothing. She would become one of the desperate street women. Lili grabbed hold of one of Midhat's toes and twisted. He moaned and writhed. Ouma raised her eyebrows in Lili's direction.

Where is it, damn you?

Blasphemy.

Lili twisted a little further and there was a small pop.

Midhat shrieked and lifted his eyes to the heavens. Allah preserve me. Fatima knows, Fatima knows. You've ruined me. My toe.

You're right, she does know.

Help me, Fatima. Help me, Midhat sobbed.

Fatima will not help you.

No, Fatima will not help you.

She is the one who told us.

Fatima has betrayed me?

You were going to betray her.

Untie me. Don't leave. Where are you going? Leave those land mines. I'm warning you. Where are you taking them? The rebels will waste them. Ha, they are nothing but nomads in a desert, trying to be a country.

Lili stared at her fingers. She had never known she had so much hatred in them. These were the fingers that ripped the chains from the Arab's dead body and these were the fingers that had twisted Midhat's toe until it snapped.

Ouma's hands closed over hers and she was propelled out of Midhat's tent and into Fatima's. The tent was dark, as always, with shadows in the corners. Ouma threw open the door so that Fatima was illuminated.

Where's the money, Fatima? Ouma demanded.

Why do you speak to me in such a tone?

Midhat said you knew. You said you knew.

I don't, I would tell you if I did. I told you about Midhat, didn't I?

Now you are lying to us.

Ouma moved restlessly around the room. Lili looked at the back of the television and shook it. She pulled at the paneling, but it was screwed on tight. And judging from the accumulated dust, it had been untouched for a while. She squinted at the couch. She pulled the cover off and gasped. It was the backseat from the Arab's Land Rover. There was even the hole in the leather, where one of his friends had dropped his cigar butt. Pieces of the Arab were strewn all over the desert.

It's in here, Ouma. Lili cleared her throat, her voice came out shaky. I am sure.

They turned the seat over and found that inside the stuffing, there were several cubbyholes dug and sacks sewn inside. They ripped out the sacks, six of them, and piled them on the floor.

What? Fatima said. Tell me what you've found.

Within seconds the sacks were upended. Piles of jewelry and stacks of money lay on the floor. Lili sorted through the gold chains and found three she thought might be hers. Or the Arab's. She put them back inside the pouch around her neck. She felt safe, her options had been returned to her.

Fatima got down on her hands and knees, shifting her palms over the ground. Her fingers tinkled through the gold, found the bracelets, chains and stones, she plunged her hands into the coins and stacks of notes. Tears fell from her eyes.

I can see, she said.

Lili peered into Fatima's eyes. They looked back at her.

I never knew, Fatima said. I never knew what was in my tent. I trusted him. All this time he was hoarding everything here, taking advantage of my blindness. This treasure has broken the curse and now that I will be the keeper of the treasure, Midhat can never leave me. Never.

Lili awoke in the morning to the sound of ranting. A man's voice rising and falling, a chant of anger and dismay. Ouma stood in the doorway.

Lili sat up and listened. What is that noise?

Midhat's a little upset that we're taking off with the land mines and two of his camels. Are you ready? The drivers arrive at midmorning. I know I'm right about this. Where's your robe and veil?

What about Midhat?

Raja and Gabriel will watch Midhat.

Raja and Gabriel? Lili raised her eyebrows.

They offered together. Strange, isn't it?

Strange, yes.

We will set the land mines together and blow them up when the drivers are in sight.

Isn't this negative publicity?

At least it's publicity. I've thought out the plan. We bring a couple of large rocks with us on the camel and we use them to detonate the land mines. A chain reaction.

Lili put on her robe and Ouma put on hers. Their eyes grew wide. Ouma's tattoo stood out as the blood drained from her face. They stared at each other unable to move their eyes, they were wearing identical robes. Identical color, design and stitch. Even the hand-made embroidery was the same. But Lili's was too tight, her shoulders were scrunched up in the air and her knees stuck out. And Ouma's was huge, it crumpled around her, hiding her hands.

Where is that robe from? Ouma demanded, her eyes dark and furious.

This is the one you gave me.

Then what am I wearing?

It's a different robe.

It's not a different robe. They are the same.

They stared a little longer and moved to the light, where they ran their fingers over each other's robes and examined the intricacies.

They are the same, as similar as two robes can be. Ouma pressed her hands over her ears. How can this be?

Ouma, this is my robe, mine from before I came to the oasis, it was made especially for me in Caza. Look, do you see the length? I recognized it the day you gave it to me.

Mine was a gift, also made for me.

From whom?

My lover.

Where did your lover have it made?

It was a gift, I didn't ask. He brought it when he came to the desert. Ouma ran her hands over her robe. But now my lover is missing.

So is . . . who . . . what did your lover look like?

He never . . . he didn't tell me. He said it was to . . . to protect me. It doesn't matter, I love him. I call him l-qamra, the moon. He is handsome and strong and this tall, Ouma held her hand way above her head. Big eyes with black camel lashes. A voice that wrapped around me, made me want—

Stop. Did he have a scar on his cheek here? Lili pointed to her cheekbone.

She looked at Lili. Ouma's lips moved, but no words came out.

Lili ran her finger along her cheekbone for several inches until it reached the bottom of her nose. Was it this long?

You? Ouma spat out the word. You were his other life? You, who he took to the big cities and bought dresses with no substance for many dirham and ate caviar and drank champagne while I was in the desert and he visited me once a month or less?

Well, Lili squirmed. I was part of his other life.

You?

We only had caviar a few times.

You?

And he had another life, too, with his wives.

Wives? I thought you were his wife.

There was no marriage. I was for entertainment.

Entertainment! And what was I?

He bought you boxes of French underwear.

A box.

He never bought me a box.

He felt guilty for leaving me in the desert. I can't stand this.

He never told me about you either.

We had plans. What have you done to him? Why isn't he here?

An image of the Arab sprawled in the sand, his hand the size of a boxing glove, wedged in Lili's mind. Her stomach constricted and she felt horribly guilty, not because the Arab was dead, but because Ouma had loved him so much and she hadn't.

We believed in the same things, Ouma's voice faltered. And . . . I left my husband . . . I can't look at you, I feel sick. You with the false hair and long bones of a stick.

Ouma whirled around the room and grabbed a knife. He used to tell me I had the most beautiful hair in the world. She began sawing at her braids, cutting off one and then sawing at the other. Lili went toward her and held out her hands.

Please, don't do that. It wasn't like that with us. You were something different to him.

Ouma brandished the knife at Lili. Stay away from me. Don't ever come near me again. Don't ever try to help me. She threw the knife at Lili. It landed softly on the rug and lay gleaming. Leave me alone.

Lili picked up the knife and left. She sat behind the tent. She dug a deep hole and shoved the knife, blade first, hard into the sand.

The Arab was Ouma's lover. The foul-breathed Arab and Ouma.

At least now she understood why the Arab never brought her into the desert, why he always left her alone in hotels for nights at a time. And why he was so desperate for her to get out of the car in the desert—Ouma.

It shouldn't matter that the Arab loved Ouma. Lili had hated him. Even so, he was her world, she had been attached to him, she had needed him desperately. What did Ouma see in him? Or what had Lili missed? Why love Ouma? Why not her?

Had the Arab forced the proud Ouma to beg on the sidewalks? Had he made her stand in a roomful of men at breast level and regurgitate everything they said to her? Had she been followed by such a terrible creature as the watchdog? Had he created her as he had created Lili? Why not her?

Moments later Ouma walked out of her tent with one braid attached. She headed to the camels, Lili following stealthily behind, ducking behind tents and palm trees.

Ouma climbed onto a camel and paused, staring out to the desert. With a heavy sigh, she nudged the camel with her heels and started off. On foot, Lili followed her into the desert where there was nothing to hide behind anymore. The air was still except for a teasing puff of air every now and then. Lili's footsteps crunched softly.

Small, tight sobs drifted back to Lili on the gentle breeze. Lili ran after Ouma, her feet pattering against the soft sand. Her toe caught on a rock and she stumbled landing on her knees. Ouma turned and halted the camel. She stared without bothering to wipe away the tears.

What do you want? she asked Lili.

I want to help you.

I don't need your help.

I know.

Ouma brought her hand up and touched her tears as if unaware of how they had come to be on her face. She looked at her wet fingers.

We are almost there.

Lili looked around. Here?

We have to go around the step dunes, to the back. The road is there, the one they will drive along.

They continued, a heavy silence descending on them until Ouma stopped the camel.

Here, she said.

Lili looked at the rusting fence, tufts of shrub and decrepit shelter. It was where she had first arrived with the Arab. The dirt track they had driven on stretched in front of Lili. She saw where he had pushed her out of the car, the fence she had climbed to escape him and the place where he had lain. It seemed so long ago, like a blurry nightmare or a story she had read several years ago.

She stared at the fence and asked Ouma, Can we also blow this up?

Ouma looked at the fence and back at her. She raised her eyebrows. If you want.

Yes, blow it all up. But this, Lili pointed to the dirt track, this is not a road.

It is a road, a desert road. Believe me, this is it. Where the cars will drive.

Where will we hide during the explosion?

The top of the dune. Ouma pointed to the rise that lay above the oasis. We duck behind it.

The land mines nestled in the wooden crate, surrounded by paper shavings. The weapons were smaller than Lili had pictured. And green, sort of cute, with a tiny body and wings that spread out from each side.

They're so small.

Like little green birds.

Green birds, Lili repeated. She looked from the box to the top of the dune. It's a short hill.

It's enough of a hill for the rock to roll. Land mines don't make huge explosions, they make centralized explosions. We scoop out small piles of sand and lay them in the holes. We throw the rocks on top and *bang*, they go off. The best thing is that they're Russian. The Russians stole their own land mines, and then we took them back.

Maybe they'll go off before.

They're not that sensitive. Sometimes these are even scattered from airplanes.

How do you know these things?

Everyone in the desert knows these things.

They saw the white dust in the air, like clouds coiling from the ground, before they heard anything. Then came the whine of the engines and, at the center of the clouds, the vehicles. Above hovered two helicopters.

Are you sure? Lili asked.

These people expect the desert to be hostile.

Okay.

Now, Ouma cried.

Now, Lili echoed, and together they pushed the biggest rock down the dune. It rolled awkwardly at first, *clunk*, *clunk*, almost stopping at times, but it picked up speed and soon bounded down the hill toward the clump of land mines. Ouma grabbed Lili's hand, pulling her down to the bottom of the dune just as the first land mine blew into an opaque wall of dust, then there was explosion after explosion, too many and Lili couldn't count them.

The sky rained sand and rocks. First the heavier pieces and then the fine bits. Lili chortled to herself, imagining the Arab's bones and the rest of the car blowing sky high.

The sand beneath her shifted and turned to liquid, she felt her body hurtling down the dune just as the rock had, sand jostling and spinning her into the center of a great wave. She tried to swim—she'd heard that in an avalanche you should swim—but her arms were pinned by the heavy sand.

Then silence. Either the whine of the engines had stopped or she was deaf. She tried to wiggle her hand and move her toes. The sand might as well have been lead, she was trapped with only grains of sand to inhale. This time she would drown in the desert.

34

At Last

THE WORLD IS WHITE WITH LOOMING SHADOWS. I COUGH. I CAN'T stop, my lungs are packed with grit. Someone whacks me on the back abruptly. I put out my hand to stop the person and find it is bound behind me, along with my other hand. Through my scratchy eyelids, I see I am propped up next to a big white van. Tied to the bumper, as far as I can tell.

People stride by, ignoring me. They are not wearing djellabas. Foreigners. To my right squats a helicopter. A man in a turban cleans the windows with a rag. A man in a spacesuit and helmet walks by. I close my eyes.

My shoulder's shake. Someone is joggling my shoulders and shouting into my ears. My body aches in dozens of ways that make my eyes focus and unfocus.

"Tell us where they are."

"You were caught in the act and damn lucky to be alive."

"What is your name?"

In front of me stands a knot of people frowning. A fat man with a florid face steps out and wields his fist in my face.

"Tell us where they are."

I don't want to talk to anyone. I want them to go away so I can sleep. Then I remember the explosions and the sand and Ouma. Where is Ouma?

My lips round to form her name, but I stop myself. I can't say her name, it would implicate her. I will take the blame. Why not? There is nothing for me to live for. I will take the blame in Russian.

"I did it," I say in Russian. "Eto ya."

The fat man stops moving his fist. "What? What did she say?"

"She's speaking in Hebrew."

"You idiot." A woman in shorts and pink freckled legs steps forward. "That's not Hebrew. I think she's speaking Russian, maybe she is a Russian. She is too tall for an Arab."

Another voice speaks up. "They are not Arabs in the desert, they are Berbers and Bedouins."

"Whatever they are, she's not one of them. It was the Russians behind it."

"Oh, God," the fat man moans. "The press has already run. The rebels have been accused, oh God. Get someone who speaks Russian."

The crowd mills around talking in low voices, casting furtive glances, avoiding my eyes. The fat man pulls out his mobile phone and yells into it.

"Get someone who speaks Russian. Now. Yes, yes, she is Russian. It was the Russians, damn them."

A man strides into the midst of the chaos and claps his hands brusquely. He is tall with light hair and fresh baby cheeks. His lips . . . his lips are oddly familiar, as if I've seen them every day of my whole life. They are stern and straight with just the right amount of arch and a nice little hollow above the top one.

"She is under arrest," he says. "I have the authority to take her immediately to Rabat, where she will be detained and charged."

Bastard. Now his lips look tight and evil and I can't imagine I thought they were nice only seconds ago. I'd love to curse at him, but I can't recall the Russian words.

"Wait one minute," said the man with the mobile phone.

"Please stand back, sir."

"I want to see your letter of permission," he declares.

"She is considered dangerous, please stand back. She could have a bomb planted on her body."

Everyone moves back several steps and then several more steps.

The evil man unfolds a piece of paper from his pocket and hands it to the man with the phone. He scrutinizes it for several seconds. The freckled lady moves in and also stares at it.

"What does it say?" she whispers to the phone man.

"How the hell would I know?" he whispers back. "Let him take her. We don't want her."

"She is Russian," the woman says.

"We are aware of that, that is why the letter is in Cyrillic."

"Right. Well, there she is. Help yourself."

The mobile phone rings. "Hello? Yes. We've rerouted the goddamn road . . . yes, the fucking Russians! I don't know . . . "

The evil man leans over and unties my hands and then reties them in front of me. He pulls me roughly to my feet and we start off down through the desert.

The desert looks different to me. In the same way that my eyes adjust from darkness to lightness, my eyes have adjusted from city to desert. The bleak paleness has become a cacophony of colors, the landscape abundant with luminescent greens, smoldering purples and shining grays. Rocks explode with color. Beneath my feet is a carpet of rich titan gold.

I can see the same desert the Arab saw, the day he told me it was heaven, not hell. Dunes slide toward me in waves of translucent mist. Plain white rocks split to reveal crystal treasures. Underneath it all are shells of intricate spirals and fossils of eyeless fish with laughing jaws and jagged teeth.

He should have told me before. Maybe I would have loved him. Maybe I would have seen what Ouma saw.

The Arab would have loved someone like Ouma, tough and fierce, believing in her land and people so strongly. I was the city to him, entertaining and superficial, glitzy and numb. Ouma was everything I was not. Natural, direct, free. Herself. I didn't have a self. My self had been in hibernation, that little green sprout encased in a thick shell.

He didn't lie to me, he just didn't tell the truth. The truth would have been that the desert was paradise for him because Ouma was there and he believed in her and he believed in the desert.

Too late, too late.

If he had lied, I would have seen it was not the truth and I would have searched for the truth. The drive for truth comes from lies.

"Ouma," I whisper.

The evil man yanks on the rope and makes me stumble. "She's fine," he says. He turns and looks nervously behind him.

I stop walking. "You know her."

"She told me."

"She told you what?"

"Where to find you."

We continue trudging to nowhere. The noise and people from the race have disappeared. I can't believe Ouma would turn me in. She pretended she had forgiven me and then she lied. The ultimate deception. I wouldn't have thought her capable of it. I am exhausted.

"Don't you have a car?"

He looks behind him again.

"How about a camel?"

"We're not going much farther."

He stops and looks around. He unties my hands. "Don't you know who I am?"

I shake my head. He rounds his shoulders and shuffles a few steps. He puts his hands around his head as if his face were hidden by a hood. I watch him.

"The lunatic?" I ask. But I shake my head again because I'm not serious.

"The who?"

I look at him, really look at him. He could be. My brain is unable to reconcile that this foreign man may be the lunatic.

"From the oasis." He taps himself on the chest. "You know me. You know me well." He looks away, embarrassed.

Now I'm embarrassed. "You can speak?"

"I decided to."

"I really thought you didn't speak," I say.

"So did Raja."

"Oh, no. You too." I study his face. "You're not a Berber."

"I never said I didn't speak or that I was a Berber. You and the others assumed it."

"Are you arresting me?"

"What?"

"The letter."

"It was the certification to the land mines. Written in Russian."

"You know."

"Ouma told me everything. I'm surprised you didn't recognize me from the beginning."

"Well, I wasn't expecting you to speak. And you shaved your beard."

I look sideways at him again. I think I can see where I bit his bottom lip in the domed tent.

"So you do know me?" he asks.

"Of course," I smile. "You're the lunatic."

"What's this with the lunatic?"

"Why were you at the oasis? Are you a spy, too?"

"I fled Marrakech. After I met you, I drank some wine with a few people I met, and the girl I sat next to was not the girl I woke up next to."

"Met me?"

"In Marrakech."

"Me?"

"I bought you tea."

My mouth drops open. I try to close it, but my muscles will not respond. My eyes drop to the blond hair on his arms, to his chest. I shake my head. I close my jaw.

"The girl insisted I honor her and marry her," he said. "Missing teeth and scrawny arms. She was not the same girl. Her brothers wanted money for the wedding and locked me in a room for days. My head hurt for three days after that night. I have no passport. No money."

"Juan's Cantina?"

My nose tests the air, taking in sharp, quick sniffs of the lunatic to see how he smells, to see if there is anything of the Arab or Ouma's husband in his scent. I inhale the remaining dust in my nose and choke.

The lunatic pounds me on the back. Now I smell him, he smells like a dog, the fresh, new skin of a puppy. And something green. He smells of grass: Bright, green-yellow grass. Very un-desert-like. The combination intoxicates me.

"Juan's Cantina," he repeats. "Yes. At first I was frightened for my life. I couldn't leave, I had nowhere to go, no money, no passport. Trapped. I hitchhiked into the desert and got off at the first oasis. I became used to living at the oasis. If I watched the camels, I was fed. It was easy." He kicks a rock that scurries along the ground. "What do you mean, you killed a man?"

"Who?"

"I don't know who. You said it."

I feel cold in the heat. "I killed the Arab," I say. It felt good to say it out loud. I square my shoulders and say it again. "I killed the Arab."

"Which Arab?"

"The one I came with."

"I thought Midhat killed the Arab."

"Midhat?"

"I saw him bury the Arab."

"Midhat buried the Arab? How do you know it was the same Arab?"

"I saw you arrive."

"Were you the one?"

"Yes."

"The dates and the water?"

"Dates?" He frowned.

"With almonds and . . . " I stop myself. I don't want to know. "Where is it now? It . . . the body?"

"The desert has eaten it long ago."

The Arab is dead. I stop and look at the desert. Really dead.

The desert is suddenly so beautiful. The velvet dunes, chameleon sky, feisty little bushes. I want to cry. I glance at the lunatic, who is watching me closely. I pull myself together.

"Why shave your beard?"

"I don't need it, I'm leaving. Ouma has given me some of the money. Enough."

"It's beautiful here," I say. I stop walking and slowly sink into the downy sand. The desert is so smooth and even though the sun is low, heat emanates from the earth as though it is alive. "Did you follow me to the oasis?"

"Yes."

"But you were there when I arrived."

"You're right, I lied. But I would have followed you."

"You lied, just like me." I stand up and we walk on. "Just like everyone."

"But now I told the truth."

"Why?"

"Why lie? I didn't follow you to the oasis. I followed you after you arrived."

"Ouma's village?"

"Both times. I felt I had to protect you, as if I were your guardian angel."

"My guardian angel," I say.

I see two things at once. I see we are walking up the road to the fence where we had planted the land mines. The dirt and sand and rocks that had been thrown about have been smoothed over by the wind so the landscape looks normal. And second, I see a lizard planted in the middle of the road.

My foot catches on a rock, I fall down in a puff of dust. There is a click. The lunatic—I can't stop calling him that—orders me not to move.

But the lizard, he doesn't scuttle away, he stays there with me. He's not frightened. He stares at me with his great eyes. I think he's the same little lizard I saw on my arrival to the desert, doing his pushups and looking at me so wisely. He is here to finally pass on his secret. He steps toward me, his tongue flicks, the ground explodes, I fly into the air, the lizard with me, he beats his eyes a few times and whispers my new name.

Thanks to:

Joe Regal for your tenacity.

Amy Scheibe for your enthusiasm.

My family for being the biggest fans of all.

And thanks to everyone I didn't name for fear of leaving someone out . . .